Also by Nicholas Royle:

NOVELS

Counterparts
Saxophone Dreams
The Matter of the Heart
The Director's Cut
Antwerp
Regicide
First Novel

NOVELLAS

The Appetite
The Enigma of Departure

SHORT STORIES

Mortality
In Camera (with David Gledhill)
Ornithology

ANTHOLOGIES (as editor)

Darklands
Darklands 2
A Book of Two Halves
The Tiger Garden: A Book of Writers' Dreams
The Time Out Book of New York Short Stories
The Ex Files: New Stories About Old Flames
The Agony & the Ecstasy: New Writing for the World Cup
Neonlit: Time Out Book of New Writing
The Time Out Book of Paris Short Stories
Neonlit: Time Out Book of New Writing Volume 2
The Time Out Book of London Short Stories Volume 2
Dreams Never End
'68: New Stories From Children of the Revolution
The Best British Short Stories 2011
Murmurations: An Anthology of Uncanny Stories About Birds
The Best British Short Stories 2012
The Best British Short Stories 2013
The Best British Short Stories 2014
Best British Short Stories 2015
Best British Short Stories 2016

SERIES EDITOR **NICHOLAS ROYLE**

LONDON

PUBLISHED BY SALT PUBLISHING 2017

2 4 6 8 10 9 7 5 3 1

First published in Great Britain in 2017 by
Salt Publishing Ltd
International House, 24 Holborn Viaduct, London EC1A 2BN United Kingdom

www.saltpublishing.com

Salt Publishing Limited Reg. No. 5293401

A CIP catalogue record for this book is available from the British Library

ISBN 978 1 78463 112 3 (Paperback edition)
ISBN 978 1 78463 113 0 (Electronic edition)

Typeset in Neacademia by Salt Publishing

Printed and bound in Great Britain by Clays Ltd, St Ives plc

FSC www.fsc.org MIX Paper from responsible sources FSC® C018072

Salt Publishing Limited is committed to responsible forest management. This book is made from Forest Stewardship Council™ certified paper.

To the memory of Alex Hamilton 1930–2016

CONTENTS

NICHOLAS ROYLE

INTRODUCTION

ONE OF MY online students, meeting me recently for the first time, told me I am much less cantankerous in person than I am online. Or in print, she could perhaps have added. Since the appearance of the 2016 volume in this series I have been publicly ridiculed by the target of a poison-tipped arrow I launched in last year's introduction. Steven O'Brien, editor of the *London Magazine*, attacked me where it hurts, i.e. online – where everyone can read it – having reacted to my criticising him for publishing his own work in the publication he edits. He didn't mention this fact in his witty takedown, which made me wonder if he did feel a little embarrassed, after all. But why should he, I'm now thinking? He's only showing that he's imbibed the zeitgeist, that he's part of the selfie generation.

He's certainly far from alone. Of the fourteen anthologies published last year that are still sitting on my desk as I write this introduction, five feature stories by their editors. Those five range from the smallest, most modest publication, put together to benefit a refugee charity, to probably the biggest, most prestigious anthology of 2016, whose editors, strangely, are not credited until we get to the title page. But then, it should perhaps be noted, there is a tendency for stories by editors, in the small sample under review, to be among the longer stories in the book in each case.

There's no getting away from the fact that 2016 was a terrible year, not only for Britain and Europe, but also America and the entire world. If we can forget Brexit and Trump for a moment, however, 2016 was a good year for the short story. Even as I make such a claim, in the light of the enormity of contextual events, it seems ridiculous to do so. In 2017, perhaps, short story writers will respond to the electoral upheavals of the previous year. Maybe they will be invited to respond, if anyone is putting together a Brexit anthology (horrible thought) or a Trump book (ugh). The themed anthologies of 2016 required contributors to seek inspiration from undelivered or missing post (*Dead Letters* edited by Conrad Williams for Titan Books), to commune with the spirit of either Cervantes or Shakespeare (*Lunatics, Lovers and Poets* edited by Daniel Hahn and Margarita Valencia for And Other Stories), to ponder the nature of finality (*The End: Fifteen Endings to Fifteen Paintings* edited by Ashley Stokes for Unthank Books), to imagine oneself an untrustworthy reporter on the capital (*An Unreliable Guide to London* edited by Kit Caless, assisted by Gary Budden, for Influx Press) or to get to grips with the big subjects of any and every year (*Sex & Death* edited by Sarah Hall and Peter Hobbs for Faber & Faber). In addition to the stories from these anthologies that are included in the present volume, I particularly enjoyed Deborah Levy's 'The Glass Woman' and Rhidian Brook's 'The Anthology Massacre' in *Lunatics, Lovers and Poets* and 'Staples Corner (and How We Can Know It)' by Gary Budden and M John Harrison's 'Babies From Sand' in *An Unreliable Guide to London*.

Unthemed anthologies kept coming, from both within genre literature (*Ghost Highways* edited by Trevor Denyer) and without (*The Mechanics' Institute Review 13*, *Bristol Short Story Prize Anthology 9*, *The Open Pen Anthology*). There were some particularly good stories in *Dark in the Day* edited by Storm Constantine and Paul Houghton (Siân Davies's 'Post Partum' nicely echoing 'Postpartum' by Louise Ihringer in *Ambit 226*), *Separations: New Short Stories From the Fiction Desk* edited by Rob Redman (David Frankel's 'Stay', especially) and *Unthology 8* edited by Ashley Stokes and Robin Jones (I loved Amanda Mason's 'The Best Part of the Day'). In an unusual project, *Something Remains* (The Alchemy Press) edited by Peter Coleborn and Pauline E Dungate, writer friends, acquaintances and admirers of the late Joel Lane were invited to take an idea or opening from Joel's notebooks and write their own story based thereupon. A lot of love, affection and homage – and good writing – is packed into the book's 400 pages; it was published in aid of Diabetes UK.

Good stories by David Gaffney ('The Man Who Didn't Know What to Do With His Hands') and Jason Gould ('Not the '60s Anymore') were the highlights of two chapbook-sized anthologies publishing competition winners from the PowWow Festival of Writing (*Stories* edited by Charlie Hill) and the Dead Pretty City short story competition (*Bloody Hull*, stories selected and with a foreword by David Mark). Charlie Hill also popped up with *Stuff* (Liquorice Fish Books), an engrossing piece that was either a long short story or a short novella and that, were the author French and his readers all French, might well have been regarded as a worthy late addition to the school of existentialist literature. Jack Robinson's beautifully written *By the Same Author* (CB editions) was in a seimilar vein, Robinson being a pseudonym used by Charles Boyle, who runs CB editions, but you never hear anyone giving him a hard time for publishing his own work.

There were fine stories in new collections from, among others, Penelope Lively (*The Purple Swamp Hen & Other Stories*), Lara Williams (*Treats*), Jo Mazelis (*Ritual, 1969*), Daisy Johnson (*Fen*), DP Watt (*Almost Insentient, Almost Divine*) and Michael Stewart (*Mr Jolly*). Charles Wilkinson's *A Twist in the Eye* (Egaeus Press) was beautifully packaged with cover art and end papers reproducing infernal visions by a follower of Hieronymous Bosch. Claire Dean's long-awaited debut collection, *The Museum of Shadows and Reflections* (Unsettling Wonder), came with hard covers and lovely illustrations by Laura Rae. The title story was one of many stories I read last year, in addition to the twenty selected, that I wish there was room for in the present volume. Anna Metcalfe's debut, *Blind Water Pass and Other Stories* (JM Originals), demonstrated her publisher Mark Richards' ongoing commitment to supporting excellent new short story writers.

Talking of which, the taste and editorial eye of *Gorse* editor Susan Tomaselli is one of the reasons why we could conceivably double the size of *Best British Short Stories* without any drop in quality. I wish I had room for stories by Will Ashon, Maria Fusco, David Rose and Bridget Penney from last year's two issues of the oustanding Irish journal. I don't know why I'm only just catching on to John Lavin's *The Lonely Crowd* 'magazine' (it's the size, format and heft of an anthology). I imagine the title character from Charlie Hill's 'Janet Norbury', a librarian, in the Spring issue, would have made sure to stock books by the title character of Bridget

Penney's 'Hugh Lomax', a forgotten novelist, from *Gorse 6*. Neil Campbell's 'The Sparkle of the River Through the Trees' was another stand-out among *The Lonely Crowd*.

It remains to be seen how the surprise departure of Adrian Searle from Freight Books will affect *Gutter*, the magazine of new Scottish writing, of which he was co-editor. No sign of any further personnel changes at *Ambit*, which published notable stories by David Hartley ('Shooting an Elephant' shared some common ground with Jenny Booth's 'I Know Who I Was When I Got Up This Morning' in *Brittle Star* 39), Daniel Jeffreys, Adam Phillipson, Chris Vaughan and Fred Johnston. I always like Emma Cleary's stories; her 'Whaletown' in *Shooter* 3, the 'Surreal' issue, was a highlight with its tumbling rocks, paper cranes and toner fade on 'Missing' posters. Gary Budden, Stephen Hargadon, Simon Avery and Lisa Tuttle contributed fine stores to horror magazine *Black Static*. I saw *Prole* for the first time even though it's published more than twenty issues (I must catch up). I enjoyed Becky Tipper's 'The Rabbit' in issue 20 and in 21 Richard Hillesley's 'Seacoal' was wonderfully evocative and affecting. With *Structo*, *Lighthouse* and *Confingo* all continuing to surpass the high standards they have set themselves – Sarah Brooks' 'Aviary' in *Lighthouse* 11 and David Rose's 'Impasto' in *Confingo* 6 being among the highlights – our best short story writers are not short of outlets for their work. My favourite John Saul story of last year, 'And', appeared in Irish magazine *Crannóg*, but *Confingo*'s 'Thirsty' was also very good.

James Wall's 'Wish You Were Here', which appeared online at *Fictive Dream*, was tight and masterful, its author completely in control of his material. *Fictive Dream* is more than worth a look for online short stories, likewise *The Literateur*. Jaki McCarrick's story 'The Jailbird' was still available on the *Irish Times* website at the time of writing and Stuart Evers' 'Somnoproxy', online at the *White Review*, is as beautifully written as his best work. On the airwaves last year, in addition to the two stories selected in these pages, Jenn Ashworth's 'The Authorities: A Modern Elegy', for BBC Radio 4, was a powerful listen.

Two things I've learned during 2016:

Almost no one, anywhere, knows how to use the semicolon; I think I do, but I'm probably wrong.

Even though I have tried to keep an open mind on the issue, I can't: 'funny' author biographical notes are never a good idea.*

The last word, last year, went to Dennis Hayward, who works on the tills at Sainsbury's Fallowfield store in south Manchester. Dennis's 2016 Christmas story was entitled 'Christmas Cottage' and raised £2500 for Foodbank, the charity having been chosen by customers of the store.

NICHOLAS ROYLE
Manchester
May 2017

* There is, in fact, one exception to this rule: the author biog on the jacket flap of the first edition of Robert Irwin's second novel, *The Limits of Vision* (1986), but it only really works with the author photo. You need to see it really.

COURTTIA NEWLAND

REVERSIBLE

LONDON, EARLY EVENING, any day. The warm black body lies on the cold black street. The cold black street fills with warm black bodies, an open-mouthed collective, eyes eclipse dark. Raised voices flay the ear. Arms extend, fingers point. Retail workers in bookie-red T-shirts, shapeless Primark trousers. Beer-bellied men wear tracing paper hats, the faint smell of fried chicken. There are hoods, peaked caps, muscular puffed jackets. There are slim black coats, scarred and pointed shoes, red ties, midnight blazers. A few in the crowd lift children, five or six years old at best, held close, faces shielded, tiny heads pushed deep into adult necks. New arrivals dart like raindrops, join the mass. Staccato blue lights, the hum of chatter. They pool, overflow, surge forwards, almost filling the circular stage in which the body rests, leaking.

A bluebottle swarm of police officers keeps the circle intact, trying to resist the flood. Visor-clad officers orbit the body, gripped by dull gravity; others without headgear stand shoulder to shoulder, facing the crowd, seeing no one. Blue-and-white tape, the repeated order not to cross. A half-raised semi-automatic held by the blank policeman who stands beside a Honda Civic, doors open, engine running.

His colleague speaks into his ear. He is nodding, not listening. He looks into the crowd, nodding, not hearing. Blue lights align with the mechanical stutter of the helicopter, fretting like a mosquito. Its engine surges and recedes, like the crowd.

The blood beneath the body slows to a trickle and stops. It makes a slow return inwards. There's an infinitesimal shift of air pressure, causing fibres on the fallen baseball cap to sway like seaweed; no one sees this motion. There's a hush in the air. Sound evaporates. The body begins to stir.

One by one, the people leave. They do not hurry. They simply step into the dusk from which they came. The eyes of adults widen, jaws drop, mouths gape and snap closed. Children's faces rise from shoulders, hands are removed from their eyes and they see it all. They crane their necks, tiny hands splayed starlike on adult shoulders.

The crowd step back. The uncertain suits, the puzzled office workers, the angry retail assistants. Chicken shop stewards, the cabbie, Bluetooth blinking in his ear. They step back until there is no one left but a trio of young men, Polo emblems on their chests, hands aloft, calling in the direction of the police.

The police shimmer and stir, lift and separate. Arms and legs piston hard, five officers backstepping faster than the crowd. They speed away from the body until they enter a parked ARV, three in the back, two in front. The vehicle gains life and roars into the distance. One of the remaining officers, a tall, gaunt woman, reels in blue-and-white tape, eyeing the young men with a glare veiled by an invisible sheen. When the tape is a tight blue-and-white snail in her hand, she also retreats, climbs inside a car with her partner, starts the engine and they roll away backwards. The visored officer joins his visored colleagues, where they gather like a bunched fist, semi-automatics raised and pointing.

The body lifts, impossibly. Ten degrees, twenty degrees, ninety; the fallen baseball cap flips from the ground, joins the head, and the man is half crouched as though he might run. He holds his left arm up, fingers reaching for sky, one bright palm facing the officers while his right hand clutches his heart. Drops of sweat fly towards his temples, as his head turns left, right. Thicker beads of red burrow into three puckered holes in his Nike windcheater, exposed beneath his fingers. He blinks one eye, as though he's winking.

He is not.

Tiny black dots leap from his chest like fleas. Three plumes of fire are sucked into the rifle barrel. He stands and raises his right hand to his blinking eye, almost wipes, and then both palms are raised. He is shaking his head. His mouth is moving fast. His eyes are shifting quickly. Streetlights turn from orange to grey.

The young man is stepping into the Civic. The police officers are stepping across the street. The Polo youths on the opposite side of the road turn their heads, beginning to brag that road man's time has come, and seconds after, of Wiley's tweets about Kanye. They're laughing. They have no idea. On the street, the young man drops his palms and crouches inside the Civic. He sits, puts his hands on the steering wheel and waits. The police officers stop shouting, they back further away. Beside the empty ARV, they lower their semi-automatics until the weapons are pointing at the dark street. Three get into the shadowed rear seat. Two climb in front. They roll backwards, away. The Polo youths reach the nearest corner. A flash of illumination from Costcutter lights, and they are gone.

The young man reaches down, starting the Civic. He puts the car in gear and its tyres turn anticlockwise, following the ARV; he could almost be in pursuit. He is not. He's looking into the rearview, chewing on his inner cheek, a habit he has learned from his mother. He's trying not to look at his blue-faced Skagen. A prickling disquiet, palms sparkling like moist earth; his hand lifts from the wheel and he marvels at this. He remembers; he must watch the road.

He wants to text his girl, but he's afraid to pull over. He wants his right foot to fall, but knows where it will lead. Yards roll beneath him, and he stops paying attention, ignores his rearview mirror. There's a song he doesn't recognise on the radio. He taps the steering wheel in time. His palms are dry. He might even be singing; it's impossible to tell. There are blue lights in every mirror. He hasn't noticed.

Noisy blue dims into black silence, but he doesn't see this either. Few pedestrians notice the ARV rolling backwards, or the baritone engine. Baseball-capped youths follow its passage, only tearing their eyes away as it leaves. Broad slabs of men duck towards the blank wall of shops, hide their faces, relax shoulders and return to upright positions. An elderly woman tries to loosen her spine, swivels too late and frowns, sensing a presence she can't quite see, pulling her trolley towards her stomach. Schoolgirls in askew blazers and stunted ties, pink Nikes and petalled socks, lift their gaze from the pavement and become grim portraiture, before they retreat into a dusty corner store. The warped door shudders closed.

The young man palms the steering wheel anticlockwise, turns left. The sad-eyed windows of unkempt houses within an inch of dilapidation. The regressive spray of thick green hoses inside a hand car wash, a dormant hearse and driver. Mustard brick new-builds and the glow of a Metro supermarket, tired women stood on corners the closer he gets to home. They try not to stare in; he tries not to stare out. He does not see the green Volkswagen van creep behind him for another half-mile. He palms the wheel left again, backs into a dead-end street. The green Volkswagen slots onto the corner of his block. He passes by its idling rumble, eases into a residents' bay, and shuts off his engine. Pats his pockets ritually to make sure everything is there. He gets out and stretches, bent backwards, reaching towards sky.

The sun on his cheeks, the occasional chilled breeze. Patchwork blue and grey above. The tinny chatter of a house radio, shouts of neighbours' kids playing football. His windcheater flutters like a flag. There is tingling warmth inside him. It's bathwater soft, soothing, and for one moment he smiles. He waves at the kids, who leap to their feet, yell his name.

Ray.

He is.

He doesn't see the man on a street corner talking into his lapel. He misses urgent eyes that scan the road and fingers pressed against one ear. The lonely intent.

He enters the house, back and further back, immersed in turmeric walls, imitation pirates' maps of back home, studio photos of himself, his mother and troublesome sister. He slows in the narrow passage. Smiles wider. His phone is pressed to his left ear, he's grinning. It makes him look younger. The phone drops into his jeans pocket. He enters the kitchen.

His mother holds him close like a promise, one hand grasping the back of his head. Her eyes are shut. She rocks him in silence, as though he were still a boy. She knows and does not know. He is muttering about being late, but she refuses to listen. On the dining table a plate is dotted with rice shards and pink slivers of curried mutton, dull cutlery laid prone, fork cradling knife, a smudged glass sentry beside them. He wrestles from his windcheater and throws it onto the back of a chair. He sits.

ROSALIND BROWN

GENERAL IMPRESSION OF SIZE AND SHAPE

I

ATTENTION SNAGGED ON the phone, lifted from flow of sentence. At window, sorry just a second, binoculars in one hand, dull light with heavy cloud, a fast dark shape with long tail, a few clean flaps and a flat glide. Checking against confusion species, especially kestrel, pigeon, collared dove and maybe even a question mark over peregrine, because after all they can fly, they migrate, never discount. All analysis done rapidly under the mind's surface, like gravel fragments collecting in underwater drift. Mouth open usually for some reason. Builds in a series of yesses, warmer and warmer, until the word surges up and breaches into clean air. Sparrowhawk.

Pre-dinner drinks in garden, chilly September, cardigans around shoulders. Then a quick movement above, face tilts back to evening sky. So does another face. Four small liquid-flying birds, forked streamers, glamorous and chasing and chattering, going south. Textbook swallows. Politely both back into the conversation.

❧

A set of well-worn routes in the brain. Necessary often for the speed of it. Something springs out of a tree and the sense of it being dark grey and long-legged and in a rush is all you've got. Or maybe an instant of a white rump in the sun and that's a certainty.

Or at the other end of the spectrum, seeing it relaxed and taking up a position in a distant bush. Too far even for binoculars, keep them up ready at face and creep forward with blind feet, hoping no sudden rough terrain. Body not dealing well with such tight control, threatens to break out in spasms, shoulders already tired. The classic nightmare, having the bins up and deciding to bring them down, or bins down and deciding to bring them up, and sometime between defocusing eyes and refocusing eyes, it's gone. Not unusual in that scenario to call a bird a wanker.

Attention goes now not only to pointed wings scaring pigeons in the market square, but also to a certain model of red Volkswagen estate, even many miles from home. Strain eyes following it away down the road. Numberplate, no.

What are you looking at? Oh, nothing.

Peregrine falcon population of UK estimated at maybe 2,000 breeding pairs. All with that look in their eye, wild alertness, tingeing into fear. One on a rock halfway down a headland in Cornwall, underline the words *also on cliffs in lowlands* in bird book and draw neat little smiley face. One hassling two golden eagles in Scottish highlands, deliriously good sighting. And one in town on the church, quick phone call and rendezvous under the spire, wow nice one, bird being photographed against its knowledge, so how are things, then leaps off its gargoyle and speeds away on its own obscure business, bugger, maybe it's camera-shy. Flash of a smile, not looking up from inspection of photos. End of lunch break, both back to offices. Watching inbox like a (ha ha) hawk after that.

Early dark morning, treading together, not speaking, cloudy breath barely visible. Sitting in the hide, serene chill water and golden reeds all around. Sun seeps in. Those important weekday times, 7am 8am 9am, melt together waiting for bitterns. At long last, utterly against expectation, one of the reeds emerges and is the thing itself, hunched and stealthy. Tiptoes, tip-talons. Breathing triumphant words, binoculars rigid with focus.

All across the county, people making coffee in morning kitchens, grubby with sleep, empty birdfeeders in gardens. Here in the hide, the construction of something else entirely, bit by bit, bittern by bittern.

Lay down thousands of sightings in your mind, build them up like a dry stone wall. A knowledge so hyper-specific it will enable you to hear the chipping from the hawthorn and not even need to think the names of robin and wren before you start to work out which one, and simultaneously listen for that otherness in the sound which might make it blackcap. Like piano exercises, get countless banalities under your belt, woodpigeons from every angle, mallards in all mutant plumages, so you're ready for the greats. The curlew in breeding season sending a long wail over drenched moorland. A vast starling murmuration suddenly contorting and bunching away from a predator and it really is a peregrine, everywhere at once, plunging in and out of the chaos. Hands placed on shoulders in the gloom and gently manoeuvring round to see a barn owl ghosting over the reeds in front of you, so definite and white, and behind you a warmth neither white nor definite.

An eagle rises above the ridge, closer than you thought it would dare, your stomach collapses, it fixes you with its bleak and alien mind.

One day perhaps will be able to glide over the top of these memories like a gannet skimming the waves, spears of pure white for wings. For now, like a blackbird foraging in dead leaves, jumping and jerking and making an unnecessary commotion.

A light lace of waxwings falls over the countryside wherever there are berries, fieldfares rattle off insults to each other, redwings are speckled and shy on the ground. And together miles and miles of road in three or four different counties, hours and hours of music on the car stereo, with attendant good-humoured arguments about bad taste. Hen harriers, pale shapes gliding wearily in to roost, and that concludes business for the day. Slow and shivering walk back to car, awkward binoculars clashing in hugs, what time do you need to be back, it's fine, she won't get suspicious for a while yet. One delicious half-hour whisky later and murmured fantasies about eloping to America, they have hummingbirds there, faces close enough to feel the heat in his cheeks, laughing at stories about swans attacking cyclists, a pub in a village whose name won't be remembered, just a straight fenland road and a huddle of houses and a camera full of photos and a mind full of dopamine. It's so strong, you know, that dopamine, it can break your arm.

2

Spring begins to force its way up, message forums explode briefly, reed warblers and sand martins and wheatears, until all arrivals accounted for. Simple pleasure of a soft greenfinch screech across an evening park. Nest-building and crazed all-day singing and territorial fly-bys from chaffinches more pink than a squashed finger. Feathery shit from willows breezing over the path, gathering in clumps. Marsh harriers courting, the renowned food pass, the female twisting herself upside down to catch the vole from her mate. Sturdy retired women into hide, depositing special lightweight telescopes, removing no-rustle coats, lifting binoculars, oh isn't that marvellous. Young fair-weather couples in denim jackets and inadequate footwear and no bins. Kids interested in basically nothing except shouting again and again the word BIRD.

Still reeling from very painful conversation which the mind insists on holding up like a banner, deserted early morning café, the guilt-pecked eyes characteristic of the adult(erous) male, so awful if she discovered, trembling and speechless, table abandoned with one empty cup and one only half-drunk. All day desolate at desk. Allowed still to be friends of a kind, accompanying each other on trips to see red-footed falcon, penduline tits, single Savvi's warbler, all rarities, feckless and exhausted and hundreds of miles out of normal range and therefore on the receiving end of hundreds of long lenses bigger than a man's face.

Collective nouns for the various developments. An

exultation of larks, certainly not. A fling of sandpipers, well, perhaps, but a bit late for that now. A charm of finches, same. A quarrel of sparrows, a confusion of guinea fowl, a pretence of bitterns, it's in there somewhere. Anyway, for official things, go through his assistant now.

Different approaches, all valid. Know all the Latin names and proper terminology, primaries, coverts, supercilium, eclipse plumage, build up an exhaustively tagged database of photos. Or read about the soft stuff, the merlin was a lady's falcon, bitterns were once hunted in fenlands and cooked in pies, red kites in Shakespeare's day were as common in filthy cities as gulls are now. Also, swifts do not land for two years after fledging, they sleep on the wing. Their reality is the spaces between things. The sight of them going in shallow circles, adding a stratum to the clear spring sky, screaming contentedly. Materialising right in front of the car, heading straight for the windscreen, before skimming up and over the roof at the last second, and two sets of held-breath laughs and one pair of hands squeezing together above the handbrake, heads turn towards each other, don't think this is a good idea, hands detach, shamefaced reluctance, it wouldn't be wise to get into that again.

Dropped off back at own car hidden on side street, first decision is whether to cry before going home, or to save it for soundless wet stretching-open of mouth later in dark bed.

Two young friends get together, both seventeen, hands timidly touching and arms around waists, watching them with real jagged thoughts inside, both with hair so translucent it's practically colourless, expressions of unadulterated, wholesome, thoroughly deserved joy.

Spin the wheel of who will receive desperate sobbing phone call today, who will dispense advice to be ignored, who will nonetheless continue to send patient and sympathetic messages. Unanimous bewilderment about why contact is being maintained, why more meetings, and yes, of course, you're right, but unthinkable to give him up, like ripping out a lark's lungs.

Those early day songs only played now for forcing relief, like turning on the tap for a stubborn bladder. Sunday afternoon in a shop, holding a shoe, raw singer-songwriter voice over the speakers, endure it perhaps, three minutes at most, thoughts winding tighter and tighter, then suddenly, no, get the fucking hell out. In the street, starlings all cocky, swinging their little shoulders and darting for bits of dropped baguette.

Paraphernalia in pockets, chocolate bar wrappers, species lists from the big reserve, gloves, unidentified plastic bit broken off binoculars, old tissue, waxy, no longer sodden.

Even more of the same, seven-hour stretches, waiting before six with the sun already high, elbows and binoculars propped on car, spotting skylarks, then the one and only red VW speedbumping into the car park, unshaven greeting, out on the road again. Or the afternoon into evening, low sun, shrieking of baby birds and glimpses of mad open mouths, cuckoos thinking about returning to Nigeria, sudden airborne squirt of shit. Then onto final destination through growing darkness, dead-end road, headlights off, coats on, jokes about being afraid of the dark and no really it is quite spooky, finding out the furious purring of nightjars.

Back in the car with completed checklist, getting on for eleven at night, no surprises when conversation turns dangerous again, pauses lengthening, voices softening. Eventually, lay-by. Making the beast with two jesus did you hear that owl. Both faces twist round to see tubby silhouette flapping away in disgust.

3

Alone for months now. Light always seems to be coming or going, always a complicated pattern of black bare twigs against a gradient of twilight sky.

Back to the nature reserve, up and down the paths, covering them all, working, writing over old memories, doing a system reset. Sky seems to proliferate with crows, a steady airborne stream arriving to roost in a stand of poplars, bickering the whole way. Large and monumental moon rises, listening to both the sounds and the silence.

Some things remain. No more joint missions chasing after rarities, or standing in perfect formation with binoculars out at contrasting angles, or turn-taking in the bushes when toilets are half an hour back that way. No more journeys home to a deadline, his deadline. No more entries in the ledger of semi-expectant goodbyes.

But still brace back on a bike to watch a sparrowhawk, still scan the skies to borderline unsafe degrees while driving, still tweet angry articles about poisoned raptors. Still load up body with clothes, head out, try to sink self into landscape, to feel whether the birds are cock-a-hoop or cowering, to listen to the robin experimenting quietly in the bushes before making its loud, two-line proclamation, then further out to silent fields and a short-eared owl, quartering the field in heavy yellow light, methodical, slow, indifferent to anything except the twitch in the grass. Being very cold and very quiet can achieve certain emotional targets, drills a hole into the chest like a woodpecker, brings its own relief.

Endure enough dragging crouching solitude, and the spring will return. Sky agitates itself with bright streaks, crocuses brace against onslaught of rain, several freezing but pleasurable drenches, birds busy everywhere, beaks sticky with nest-building. One day find self in late-night park, not out of the ordinary these days, furniture too unmoving, overgrown wet grass and black bulks of cows vastly preferable. Somewhere behind uneven masses of trees, lights of houses, the incomprehensible lives of other people.

Longing for a nightingale, endless invisible voice in the night, on and on bubbling out trills and whistles, a bombardment of ideas, and a single adjective in the bird book, song variable, those stolid ornithologists, implausible is more like it. But no nightingale. Waiting for nightingale like waiting for miracle.

One day in the sun a scratchy song, flicker of bird into bush, dunnock or linnet or whitethroat, disappears, will never know, a fist tightens in the stomach, no more of his instantaneous expertise. But it passes, it passes, the world settles again.

A wave of birds rising from a tree, automatically look round, what are they afraid of, several long inconclusive seconds, head cranes right back, far-off seagull, nothing else in sight. Only me.

GISELLE LEEB

AS YOU FOLLOW

IT IS A bold entrance. You cannot miss it, booming out its yellow lights and buxom barmaid cartoon, across from the magnificence of soaring glass. It has beer, beer, beer and other things besides, if you have the money.

Down the stairs, out of the soft end-of-October rain and Halloween nearly over. You duck under the low arch, burly bouncers stopping you, pointing out a far bench, changing their minds, pointing out another, squeezing you in beside a quiet couple picking at something green, out of place among the shouting and singing, the plates of left-over Bratwurst and chips, the men standing and cheering on the boys in lederhosen, with their brass instruments, their paid smiles, to keep going and going and the long wooden trays of spirits, red shots lined up in sixes and twelves, and on one end a sparkler to set them going, to light the spirits before dawn, and they go down down down and light up the insides. And the felt hats all new-looking, hired, and the voices on and on, louder.

It is ten o'clock and the jackets are thrown over chairs, over benches, forgotten, and what should hurt the ears is pure music through this veil of spirits. And the beer steins, two pints, the biggest glasses you have ever seen in London Town, all the way from Germany.

It is almost the end of Oktoberfest and it is the thirty-first, the barmaids, white aprons streaked with fake blood, pushing through the cobwebs with more flaming trays as a group of men stand and they are going drink, drink, drink, as one of them holds a glass up to his lips and churns his throat, head back.

And next to him you see a child, blue eyes and blond hair, fashionable short back and sides, and he is pointing his young thumbs, beckoning the band closer, suggesting a song and clapping hard as it starts up. And him, him, him, he points. And he is too young to be here, you say to your friend. But the boy is swaggering, confident, he is dressed like the men, in tight-fitting, dark-blue trousers, a pinstriped shirt, and he is happy, happy, he is pure joy this boy, this very young man.

Perhaps he is with his dad, you say to your friend. But it is ten o'clock on Thursday in London Town and he is the brightest of them all. And when the spirits come again, he is plucking the sparkler from the tray and he is holding it in his teeth and sparks are flying from his mouth as he sweeps his head and they are cheering and laughing, they are ruffling his hair.

And he must have had a few sneaky ones, you say, but the young can get drunk, so drunk, on pure joy, you think, and you remember how your cheeks shone without the help of anything when you too were young.

And the band is beaming, they are all young too, but not as young as the confident boy. And he is pushing the spirits along the table, he is leaping up and changing places and steadying a big man in his seat as he lunges forward and crashes into the table and the spirits jolt and then are still.

And the group stand to dance, swinging their arms to the

music. And tonight it is Thursday, tonight they are men and the day is gone and they are held out of time in this place below the street level, held in its swaying lights and merry shouting.

And you cannot keep your eyes off this boy-man, you cannot believe that he can be so bold. You imagine him begging his dad to let him come. And his mother, you think, does she approve? You imagine him remembering this night forever in the future, the night he was one of the boys, the night the world first blazed with glory for him, the night he was a true man.

But he plays his part so flawlessly, you cannot imagine a young boy like this, unless he is very drunk. And you look closer and you see in front of him, in front of the spirits lined up, in front of the biggest glass of beer that you have ever seen, you see a glass of water.

And you long to ask someone how old he is, but you hesitate to break the spell, you hesitate because Christmas has come early, you are in a magic place, you are remembering dancing all night before you ever drank a drop, you are remembering how pure the world is, you are remembering beauty and truth and how it was before you came to this place, to this theme bar for pleasure.

And you are nearly done with your first pint and you find that you are tapping your foot to the oompah music, the corners of your mouth pulling up, and your friend is smiling as you both stare at the boy and it is too loud to speak, and you see the imp gesturing to the bar again, another tray arriving, another sparkler showering sparks from his mouth and you think he looks like an arrogant son of kings. He cannot possibly be a boy.

And you nod at your friend and you point to a two-pint beer stein on the next table and he signals the waiter - whose accent is in fact German - and you order two of the big glasses and you sit and watch the boy-child as they ruffle his hair, as one of them puts his arms around him, another slides him along the bench, for he is small and slender and light as a feather.

And you long for a tray with a sparkler, but there are only two of you.

And one of the men stands and, 'Are you going, are you going?' the elf shouts and you both hear his voice and it is a man's voice and you think, finally, that he must be a man.

And then his eyes catch yours and he is pointing at you and your friend and he comes round the table and he is laughing and he is slamming down two shots and his thumbs are pointing at the band and they strike up a song and you are both laughing, throwing back the red spirits, and when you look up the sparkler is in his mouth again and you feel as if your head is flying along with the sparks and you are standing and dancing, you are standing with the young imp and he is shouting, play a song, play a song, and the music is inside your head and you are young again, you are at your first wedding, you are drunk, and you cannot believe that it has arrived, this life, the life you have waited for all those years while you were growing up.

And the bell rings and the boy takes a sparkler. The men at the table are standing up and he is leading them out the door, shaking hands with the bouncers, and he is beckoning to you and your friend and you get up and follow, laughing and cheering as you stumble across the cobblestones, past Smithfield Market, all shuttered up, past Bart's, gates locked, past the silent dome of St Paul's, down to the river, to the mighty Thames.

It is mild for the last day of October and the moon is bright and the tide is high, the waves swelling and full. And beside the river wall, the men light fags and you do too and you feel like you are in your past and you draw deep and the sparks are replaced by the moon flitting off the crests of the waves and you stare out at the stumps of the old bridge, the waves touching it with a kiss before they move under the new bridge next to it, and then on.

And the lamps on the river Thames are burnishing your eyes, burning and burning your spirit-filled eyes. And you have tears in them now as you look at the young elf, laughing, laughing like quicksilver, and you watch him darting through the chattering men as they smoke fags and throw them into the dirty water. And he leaps onto the wall, laughing, bending over the waves, and they do not see him, they do not see him as they light their cigarettes and the moon swims in their eyes.

And you look at the men and back at the wall and there is only a stone cherub sitting well above the tideline, its expression hidden from you, its chubby arm pointing towards the dark river behind it. And you go closer, you hesitate, but you haul yourself up and you lean on the stone shoulder, catching your breath, lighting another fag.

And you look into the water and you cannot take your eyes off your reflection, a boy in shirtsleeves, young and slender, bursting with pride and with joy, the sparkler in his mouth arching bright flashes over the swelling river.

And you hesitate, you hesitate, but you follow him in, gasping with life at the freezing water, laughing as the bright light stretches, then folds itself below the spirited waves, laughing as you follow him down.

Laughing, until you look up and now the light is dancing far above your head. And you reach for it, desperate, you kick up, but a small hand is dragging you into the dark and as you are pulled down, the waves whispering, the waves whispering and moving on.

JAY BARNETT

AREA OF OUTSTANDING NATURAL BEAUTY

I ASKED MUSHY if he had the waterproofs. He had no idea what I was talking about.

'Borrow mine.'

I handed him the sleeves. He held them out in front of him and stared at them blankly.

'Just put your arm in, and clip it to that thing there,' I said, pointing to the thing.

I was in no mood for traps. My sister had visited the night before, came with a bottle of brandy bought from a man at Hornby Dock. It had been five years since I'd tried the stuff. I must have had half the bottle to myself.

Mushy managed to get the left sleeve on but I had to help him with the right. I had him check the traps by the brook. That way I could sit and do nothing while he learnt something.

'You done your water training?' I asked him.

'This is my water training, isn't it?'

'It is now.' I took a step towards the brook. 'It's easy. You know how to check a trap?'

'Yeah.'

'Well, see that marker?' I gestured to a triangle at the brook's edge, fluorescent orange in the long grass.

'Yeah.'

'There's a trap in the water just under there. There's four along here.'

He looked along the bank, at the bright triangles every thirty metres or so.

'Just see what colour the light is on them traps. You might have to get your arm in to shift whatever shit might be clinging to them.'

He lifted his hands to look at the rubber sleeves.

'If the light's red, leave it. Green, give us a shout.'

As I walked to the others sat on the shingle, I looked over my shoulder at Mushy.

'They won't be full!' I shouted. 'They prefer open water.'

Jennifer sat cross-legged, her arms propped behind her. I lay out flat next to her and looked at the sky.

'Bright,' I said.

Bykes paced up and down a few metres away, trying to get a signal on his radio. He always brought it with him; it could pick up communication bands as well as commercial signals. He liked to listen in on the monitoring depots dotted around the coast, hoping to hear of things washed up, discolouration, suspicious water levels. For the most part it was talk of the weather, the tide and the safety of distances. After a while he would tune out to find something with more song about it. He walked towards us and spoke over the music on his radio.

'St Louis knows about the milk.'

The chill of the morning had faded and the backs of my legs were beginning to sweat against the shingle. I looked around for something to drape over my eyes, a cloth, a bag, anything.

'You listenin'?' said Bykes.

'What?'

'St Louis knows about you stealing milk.'

'Bullshit! We all steal milk.'

'And soap. And sweetener. And toilet roll,' said Jennifer. 'But it's you an' milk that got the mention.'

This was rich coming from her.

'Where've you heard this?' I asked.

'Depot. Last night,' said Bykes. 'Steve told me. Said he heard from horse's mouth.'

'Fuckin' Steve.'

At the bottom of my pack I found a clean entry-rag. I draped it across my eyes and lay back down on the shingle. I arranged myself on the stones with tiny shimmies, trying to mould a small dip to rest in. Once I was comfortable, I stilled myself and listened to the brook.

'You'll be all right,' said Jennifer. 'Just lie your way out of it.'

'Fuckin' Steve,' I said.

'You're not gonna drag us down if they fire you, are you?' asked Bykes.

I didn't answer, just listened to his radio. An advert about giving blood, an advert about land insurance, something about food. A song came on that reminded me of school days and of the Fenton Recreation Ground on winter nights. We used to drink cider there, and smoke, and scratch our names in the see-saw. It was fun until the older boys started bringing airguns along. They fired in the dark, aiming at the sound of laughter by the swings. A well-placed shot would break the skin.

I struggled up from my recline in search of something to drink. Over by the brook I saw Mushy starting back, his rubber arms held out by his sides.

'All empty!'

We gathered our things up from the shingle. Mushy unclipped the waterproofs and passed them to me.

'Keep them till they're dry,' I said. 'Don't want them wettin' my bag up.'

'Where'm I supposed to put them?'

'Stuff them through your belt.'

With no great urgency we walked towards the overgrowth. Somewhere in there were traps Forty-Nine to Seventy-Two. Our boots had trodden the path more days than not for the past fifteen years and now a dark arch welcomed us where weeds and wildflowers should flourish. We passed through and edged down into the path. 'This is Dog Holloway,' I said to Mushy.

The holloway was a quarter-mile long on a slight gradient; to walk it west, as we did, meant downhill. It was an ancient, dank place no wider than three metres across. Either side, mud walls reared above our shoulders, while trees formed shelter overhead.

'Why's it called Dog Holloway?' asked Mushy.

'Don't know.'

He looked to the others for answers. Jennifer shrugged. Bykes wasn't paying attention.

We walked down the holloway towards the first trap. It was burrowed into the bank so that it was flush with the earth. The indicator showed empty so we moved on to the next. There were six altogether, laid and set in the mud walls. Bykes was between stations on the radio, filling the narrow space with white noise. He settled on something old and tried to whistle to it. He didn't know the song.

The second trap was in darkest shade, nestled in the roots of a stump. We couldn't see the indicator for a thick web that had formed over it. Jennifer put her gloves on to pull it away.

'Wasn't here Tuesday,' she said.

Her hand knocked a root and some loose soil fell away. Beneath it the very earth seemed to move with millipedes and woodlice. The creeping things were in good number. She removed the web. Underneath it the light was red.

'Are they mostly empty, the traps?' asked Mushy.

'Pretty much. They don't like our bait,' said Jennifer. 'The only thing they like is . . . well, you know. And nutmeg, of course.'

Jennifer bought nutmeg a few years ago from a pop-up in Camber. It cost her a month's rent. 'Christmas isn't the same without it,' she'd said, then managed to sell some at a premium back at the depot. A sprinkle goes nice in the traps.

We walked the rest of the holloway without fuss, glancing at the indicators as we passed. All lights red.

We came out into the opening by Kingsley Bank, where the Hide is. The sun hit us flush, quite something from the cool dark of the holloway. Jennifer unzipped the top half of her suit, down to the vest, to let her arms warm in the glow. Somewhere a few miles away we heard three intermittent bursts. Probably the guys over in Heathfields, messing with charges. They're meant to blow holes in the ground for new traps, but they wouldn't have been laying new traps. Who'd waste time laying new traps?

'Fucked up,' I said. 'They're gonna try me for milk, while that lot steal explosives?'

It was easy to steal from the store. Tell one of the old boys you need a form then go in and take a bomb. We once strapped six charges to the base of a young beech tree. When it blew it left the ground and near flipped three hundred and sixty degrees.

'Milk?' asked Mushy.

'You'll not need to pay for milk again,' said Jennifer. 'Just take it from fridges at the depot.'

'None of you'll be taking anything if they do me,' I said.

The Hide sat twenty feet above the forest floor, built on eight great legs of cedar pine. It was a place humans could hide from nature, built for the days when people watched birds. It was closed to the public years ago, then used by our company for research by night. It's used for nothing these days. Night work was cancelled indefinitely after Longden Lane. The Hide had become unfit for purpose, left to the elements. We weren't meant to go near the thing but would always use it to sit out the rain, or the wind, or the job. Wasn't much point in heading up that day, the weather was too nice for the shade of the Hide. I decided to show Mushy anyway.

We took to the steps, waterlogged and soft underfoot but still equal to the weight of a man. The trees had become so unruly that some branches reached in through the viewing points. Mushy grabbed at one and shook it. My walkie-talkie let out two short blips, the sound it makes when the batteries are dying. I leant out of the north opening and looked down. Jennifer was poking the ground with a small knife.

'I got the beeps!'

She looked up from whatever fungus she was probing, then at the walkie-talkie on her belt.

'Well I haven't.'

Down through the trees I could see patterns in the dirt, traces of them. Thin, entwined markings circling trees or heading direct into outcrops of bush. I could also make out three traps, all of their indicators red.

I turned around to see Mushy half leaning out of the south viewing point. He was facing up towards the sky with his back resting on the timber frame. With both hands he grabbed at something out of sight and, with a pull, disappeared through the opening. I walked quickly towards him, looked through the gap to see nothing but blue sky.

'Proper sunny up here!' he shouted.

None of us had ever climbed onto the roof of the Hide. I could hear Mushy testing the timber's strength above me. His body moved and the wood creaked. No one saw to the maintenance of the thing. Its rivets and joists moaned in the damp. One day it would give up.

'I'm going down, Mushy. Be careful.'

Jennifer stood by a tree, a limp thing, its leaves unseasonably dry. She dragged a scraper along its bark and it came away like paste. She put it to her nose and grimaced. Bykes was sat on a mud mound in the dappled shade, his suit half undone for the heat of the day.

'All empty here,' I said, 'but I couldn't see Fifty-Eight's.'

Bykes stood up, stretched his arms overhead.

'I'll go check it.'

I sat and leant against a cedar leg. Lots of leaning. Lots of sitting.

'Is he safe up there?' asked Jennifer, nodding towards Mushy.

'Probably not.'

I took the batteries from my walkie-talkie then rubbed them in my hands. I switched their positions, as if tricking the device that they were new. It killed the beeps at least.

From beyond the sound of the leaves, Bykes yelled over.

'There's a half in here!'

I pulled myself up from the forest floor using the cedar leg as grip.

'Mushy! Come down and see this.'

The three of us made our way to Bykes. He was stooped by the trap, prodding it with an extendable baton.

'Well, it's half of sumit,' he said, 'but not half of what it's meant to be.'

Some mammal or other had sniffed out the bait. It was hard to tell what it was, now gelatinous and tangled. Bykes poked at its innards; they were moist and reflected the sun. He cleared the mess then I had Mushy reset the trap. He forgot about the bearings but I didn't correct him, and I didn't care. We still had the Holes and Bonisall. Damn Bonisall. We moved on from the Hide, the midday sun on top of us.

'OK, Mushy,' I said. 'These are the Holes. If there's anything caught, it's likely caught here.'

The foxes had long gone but their holes were still used, so much so that the ground had hollowed out and taken on a spongy honeycomb effect. A run of dips and mounds, dry in open air. Nothing grew at the Holes. Bykes stood at the edge of the area, the forest behind him and the blue sky in front.

'Shame to waste the sun checking traps,' he said, then peered into one of the small dark openings. Down there was trap Sixty-Two. Behind him, a great buddleia loomed tall as a house, heavy with cones of white flowers. He squinted and cocked his head left.

'Gonna need to shift this a little. Can't see it.'

He picked up a stick from the forest behind him, then shoved it from sight, down into the hole of trap Sixty-Two. He appeared to be exerting some degree of force down there; at times it looked a struggle. Jennifer, Mushy and I looked on. Tired. Not bothered. Hot. We'd all unzipped the top halves of our suits. Bykes wedged the stick to a satisfactory point then planted his feet either side of the hole and pulled. And pulled. And we watched. Mushy spat on the floor and Jennifer wiped her brow. Then Bykes pulled some more, pulled until the stick broke free and he fell straight back, right into the buddleia. The whole thing wavered, shaking loose from its flowers a swarm of butterflies we hadn't known were there. Maybe a thousand, the colour of milk. They fluttered into our group and bounced around our packs, some stopping on the damp of our skin to taste the salt then move off. As they flew in and about us we held our arms out from our sides, as if swimming in phosphorescence. Most returned to the buddleia, others to the forest behind; some took to the sky above the dry, open Holes. They had dispersed to less than a quarter when Mushy reached out and grabbed a straggler in his fist. He held tight then opened his palm to look at it.

'Dust,' he said.

Bykes was still by the hole in the shadow of the buddleia, looking down at trap Sixty-Two. The stick must have worked because he looked up and said: 'Empty.'

There were three more at the Holes. Trap Sixty-Three was empty. Trap Sixty-Four was empty. Trap Sixty-Five was empty.

'Fucking Bonisall,' I said.

I looked at the others.

'Let's sit here a while.'

Jennifer lay burning her face in the heat. Mushy walked about, testing the strange terrain underfoot. He stopped by every hole to spit down into dark. Bykes sat on his knees, his legs tucked under his bum. He tuned into a monitoring depot over on the coast, the faint sibilant voices of people at work. We lay in the sun picking up fragments of conversation. Some fault in an engine room near the Hanagan Channel. It was solved, apparently, by the push of a button.

There were two ways to Bonisall. Through the Mess, or up Chorley Way. The Mess took fifteen minutes, maybe less. An overgrown place rank with dangerous weeds, the sort that weep and hurt the skin. We had our suits for such things but it was so nice in the sun. Chorley Way was the longer path. A flat track of mostly dirt. There were no traps on either route. The Mess was considered too poisonous. Chorley Way, too flat and open either side. Most days we took the Mess, quickest option preferred. Bykes began to zip up. He looked at Mushy.

'You got goggles?'

'Think so.'

I stared at the tangled entrance to the Mess, considered the relative dramas in there. Then I looked east towards Chorley Way. As plain a track as I'd known.

'Let's go Chorley Way,' I said.

'Don't be stupid,' said Bykes.

I grabbed my things up and moved east.

'I'm going Chorley Way.'

Jennifer rubbed her goggles with a rag. She frowned at me. 'You'll hold us up.'

'That's the idea. If we get back to the depot a bit later, maybe St Louis will have gone home already.'

'I got no problem with St Louis,' she said. 'It's not me he wants.'

'Let it be known. If this St Louis bollocks is true and I'm dragged over the coals, I'm naming names.'

The three of them looked at me. Jennifer put her goggles back in her pack.

'You're a bastard.'

'True,' added Bykes.

Mushy said nothing.

I'd forgotten the charm of Chorley Way. Just some fields with a path running through them. Sometimes dirt, sometimes tarmac. So flat and open is the route, that its skies are big. They are empty, but they are big. If we were to see a bird on the job, it would be there. I walked purposely slow, turned twenty minutes into thirty. The others walked ahead, eventually out of sight. I thought about what I might say if confronted by St Louis: *Shit job anyway.* I walked on, burnt my skin a little along the way. I saw no birds.

By the time I got to Bonisall they had checked all traps. Empty, of course. The three of them, perched by the truck, waiting. Seph sat with his leg out the driver's side door. He was the depot's oldest driver; a fat man, more gum than teeth.

'Milky, milky,' he said, as I walked from behind the silo.

The Heathfields lot were on the truck.

'Hey up, Mushy!' one of them said. 'Was Jenny good to you?'

He must have trained with them earlier in the week. After us, he was likely on to Canton. Poor bastard. At the start of it all.

I sat alone at the seat without windows. As we moved off there was nothing to look at but the inner wall of the truck. It was covered in coarse polyester lining, warmer than glass to rest against for sleep during transit.

Chorley Way hadn't helped, St Louis was still at the depot. All I could do was avoid eye contact. There were thirteen minutes left on the clock and he wanted to make sure no one left early. I filled in my day's report form. Nothing to report. I moved my pen across the sheet, circling the same marks I'd already made just to eat up the time. I looked across at the others doing the same.

'Can I have a word?'

It was St Louis. I pretended not to hear. Kept my eyes on the sheet. Circling. Circling again.

'Yeah, no worries,' said Mushy, and went into his office.

Jennifer, Bykes and I looked at one another.

'What's that about?' asked Jennifer.

'Maybe our Mushy's a spy,' said Bykes.

I tossed my report form in the pigeonhole; it was still attached to the clipboard.

'Now's as good a time as any to get out of here.' I hurried to the changing rooms.

I was down to civvies in record time. I looked at my watch. Two minutes past finish. My hands were filthy. I'd wash them at home. I grabbed my bag and went to leave through the fire exit.

'There you are!'

St Louis, the bastard. He'd appeared like a ninja; sly. He walked up close, my back against the steel of the locker. His tie tangled with a lanyard proudly displaying name and title: *Daren Bell. Enickford Department Supervisor*. Can't remember why we called him St Louis. Bell-end would have been better.

'Can I have a quick word?'

He had me enter his office first. A stuffy little place; tiny high windows. A pile of boxes stacked in the corner concertinaed under their own weight.

'Sit down,' he said.

The chair was surprisingly comfy; static, without wheels. I scanned his desk. He was the only person in the company to bring a briefcase to work. It sat with his keys on top. Next to that was a carton of milk.

'You're in the frame,' he said.

My trapping days were up. The land of milk and sunshine crumbled all about me.

'You know Don's leaving at the end of the year?'

'What?'

'Don. He's off in November. It's likely they'll be shifting up top. I'm looking at his position, which leaves this desk free.'

'Oh.'

'You're in the frame.'

'The frame?'

'For my position. This position. I put your name forward.'

I stared at the milk carton. Judging by its moisture it'd not long been taken from the fridge.

'Just had John in here. Said he liked training with you the best.'

'John?'

'The lad. Said your team's the best.'

'Cause we do nothing.

'Well, what do you think?'

My elbows were on the armrest, hands interlocked across my belly.

'About what?'

'About this, sitting here.' He tapped the desk. 'You'll not be getting out in the sun as much, but you'll not be getting out in the rain, either.'

I couldn't take my eyes off the milk, fresh out the fridge and sat by his briefcase at home time. The bastard was stealing the stuff.

'I'll give it some thought,' I said.

'Better pay, too.' He opened his briefcase, threw his keys in, then looked at me across the desk. 'You can go now.'

The depot was silent. Everyone had cleared out, off home for teas and beds. I stood washing my hands in the boot sink. *St Louis. St Louis.* What nickname would they give me, should I become supervisor? I watched the day's mud swirl the porcelain. Quite the gyre. Funny, really, all that dirt for so little work.

ANDREW MICHAEL HURLEY

WHILE THE NIGHTJAR SLEEPS

AFTER THE RAIN, the last of the daylight came riding over Mynydd Mawr with the crows. The mountain choked on torrents of white water and the bracken smelled of its colour. From the shadows of the sycamore tree, the old horse emerged and nibbled at the edges of the puddles. The world had awakened again just in time for dusk.

'We'd better go now,' said Mr Davidson. 'Before it goes too dark. Do you think the boy's up to it?'

He was joking, of course, and everyone laughed. It had already been decided that this year he would be allowed to go with Mr Davidson to the woods and then stay up late. He was twelve years old now. He wasn't a child any more.

They crossed the field to the trees and the horse looked up at them, its head and the darkening clouds and the racing crows reflected in the water.

Autumn had passed through the valley like a sickness, turning the bramble fruit into wizened pellets, wilting the hogweed. Everywhere there was a smell of rot and deadfall.

'Keep your eyes peeled now,' said Mr Davidson. 'He'll be here somewhere.'

'Who will?' said the boy.

'You'll know when you find him.'

They set off along the fringe of the trees, where he'd watched Mr Davidson earlier in the day scattering red dust into the air. Working methodically, they lifted up the bracken and rooted under fallen branches.

By now, at the Davidsons' request, the boy would normally have been sent to his bedroom to play with his toys. He had only ever been able to watch from his window and guess what the red dust was for or what Mr Davidson found at the tangled hem of the wood. His mother would never tell him.

'When you're old enough you'll understand,' she said.

Well, now he was.

They searched for several minutes, Mr Davidson singing to himself, until the boy found a dead nightjar under a thicket of ferns.

'No, not dead,' said Mr Davidson. 'He's only sleeping. Go on. Don't let him get cold now.'

The boy wiped his hands on his jeans and crouched to pick up the bird. It was still warm. Its head dangled.

Mr Davidson handed him a tea towel and the boy swaddled the bird and carried it back to the cottage at arm's length. They all laughed at him when he brought it into the kitchen. There was always laughter when Mr and Mrs Davidson came with their friends. Laughter was good, they said. Laughter was the key. A beacon.

'Don't listen to them,' said his mother, holding him to her chest in a charade of protection.

She kissed him on the forehead and the others ruffled his hair and patted his shoulder. The boy found himself smiling at the congratulations.

'Perhaps that means it'll be your turn this year,' said Mrs Davidson as she took the bird from him and laid it in an enamel basin next to the woodstove.

'Who was it last time?' said Mr Davidson. 'You know my memory.'

A rheumy-eyed mole of a man coughed and put up his hand.

'And before that it was Ruth,' said Mrs Davidson.

'It was Ruth two years on the trot,' another voice said.

'Well, that's how it is sometimes,' said Mr Davidson. 'Everyone will get a turn eventually.'

'Here now,' said the mole man, touching the boy on the arm. 'I'll tell you the story of the nightjar,' he said and the others moaned like cattle.

'Now, come on,' said Mr Davidson, pretending to scold them. 'He has to tell it, you know that. Tradition is tradition.'

The others laughed and someone poured the mole man a glass of beer.

'Now see, the nightjar,' said the old man, cleaning his glasses on his sleeve, 'he was once a great hunter, better than the hawks and the eagles. He didn't live in the woods like he does now; he went out over the mountains looking for the hare and the wild cat.'

One day, the mole went on, there was a thunderstorm and the nightjar flew down to the woods for shelter and found every creature asleep. The King of the Wood had fallen in love with a beautiful dryad and had dusted the trees with a potent pollen. Then he could dance with her without the Queen finding out. But when he saw that the nightjar was awake and watching, he took away his sharp beak and his talons and forced him to chase after moths in the dusk.

'But while the nightjar sleeps,' said the mole, 'it dreams of what it used to be and still sees beyond what isn't true. And so can we, if we choose to look.'

He grinned at the boy and lit a cigarette and drank some of his beer. In his younger days he had been in the navy and had tattoos on his hands.

'Life doesn't end,' someone else said, and the rest of the table murmured their agreement in words to that effect, including the boy's mother, which surprised him. She had never believed in God. Perhaps that was what she'd been keeping from him. Perhaps these people had turned her.

There were a dozen of them around the table. All from the village that sat in the valley below, its roofs like wet coal, the chimneys linked by brown smoke. It was where the Davidsons now lived, the cottage having proven too much for his lungs and her hip.

They were all dressed in their best clothes. The men were clean-shaven and wearing ties, the women clownish with rouge and lipstick that the boy didn't think they wore very often.

They'd been so kind, his mother was fond of telling people back in Sheffield. Such compassion. Such goodness.

A few years earlier, the boy's father had died suddenly and while they'd carried on coming back to Llygaid Finiog every October, reckoning on it being nothing more than a quiet pilgrimage of remembrance, these people from the village had become like a family. They were the proof that even the darkest moments in life were only junctures that led to somewhere better.

So his mother said. Without his father here, the boy found

it dull and miserable. The rooms smelled like the water that came off the mountain and boredom seeped into everything like damp. He wore the fun out of the toys and books he brought with him after the first day and the picture on the tiny television set was always tugged in the middle, as if someone had drawn their finger through a wet painting. When the Davidsons and their friends came over he both enjoyed and hated the intrusion. He wanted them to leave and yet he wanted to know what they laughed about downstairs.

He'd never quite known what to make of the people from the village. Every year when he and his mother and father had come to stay in the cottage, they'd drift up in ones or twos bringing firewood or horse feed, or be sent by Mr and Mrs Davidson to fix this or that. Or come just to be nosy, his father had said. His mother had called him curmudgeonly but without much scorn in her voice. She knew what he meant. They were odd little people, the Davidsons included. Like him, she'd laughed at the way they'd lent them their tastes along with the cottage – the porcelain dogs, the huge cutlery. But now she seemed glad they were here, cradling her, soothing her. They'd all lost someone. They all understood.

They ate in the kitchen and they filled the boy and his mother in on what had happened in the village since their last visit. There'd been floods in the spring; Tom Evans' ram had got loose; Mrs Hurt had cancer. But the boy didn't really listen and he wasn't hungry. He was too excited to know what was going to happen. Excited and yet open to the possibility of disappointment. There was every chance that the rest of the evening would just be an extension of the conversation around the dinner table and that the hysterical laughter he'd heard downstairs all these years was due to nothing more than the effects of beer and wine. If that was the case he'd know for certain what he'd suspected for some time: that things were never as good as they promised to be.

The dusk fell quickly and mist ghosted across the horse's field. When it went dark everyone gathered in the small front room and his mother closed the curtains. They talked for so long that the boy felt himself drifting into sleep, wedged and warm as he was between the plump woman who liked to mother him more than his mother and the man with a paste-brush moustache who smelled charred with pipe smoke and spoke no English.

The nightjar had been brought in from the kitchen and lay asleep in the bowl on the hearth.

When the clock chimed the hour, Mrs Davidson took hold of her husband's hand and the others joined theirs and a circle formed around the room. Perhaps they were going to pray, thought the boy. Perhaps these people were evangelists. He'd once seen a programme on television about a church in America where people laughed and laughed until they fell into spasms on the floor, dribbling with joy.

'Close your eyes now,' said Mrs Davidson and everyone did as she asked.

The plump woman's hand was damp. The man – the Sergeant, the boy called him – had a surprisingly soft grip.

The room fell silent apart from the pop and split of the wood on the fire and the rain that had returned to the valley and caught the windows. He felt the plump woman breathing next to him; the Sergeant cleared his throat.

'Look for them now,' said Mrs Davidson. 'Those that have left our sight.'

Around the room, people shuffled themselves comfortable. They sat still for a long time (were they Quakers, then? the boy wondered), until the silence was broken by the plump woman next to him. Her body was shaking, her hand tightening on his as she began to laugh.

It spread quickly through the others, increasing in volume, coming in waves like the rain; a burst and then a trickle before another barrage filled the room. Still holding the boy's hand, still with his eyes closed, the Sergeant wiped away tears from his cheeks.

Now Mrs Davidson fetched the enamel bowl and passed it around the circle. Everyone touched the nightjar, laughing harder as they stroked its feathers. When it came to the boy he could feel that it was still as warm as it had been when he'd lifted it from the grass. He pushed his fingers deeper into the down of its belly, feeling its heart softly trilling, the muscles of its wings beginning to stir. And then the bowl was taken from him by the Sergeant who put the bird to his cheek.

While they were all still laughing, Mrs Davidson touched the boy's mother on the hand and nodded. His mother began to cry and called the boy over and held his face.

'It's us,' she said. 'It's our turn this year.'

'Go on, now,' said Mrs Davidson. 'The nightjar will be awake soon. There isn't much time.'

They went out of the room into the cold hallway. The boy could hear the Sergeant and the plump woman laughing loudest of all.

'Don't be frightened. It's what brings them here,' said his mother. 'Wouldn't you come into the cottage if you heard people laughing?'

It didn't seem like a question he was supposed to answer

and she led him past the ticking clock and the ugly gold mirror.

'We have to go to the end room,' his mother said. 'That's where they always wait.'

The boy followed her reluctantly.

'Don't you want to see him?' said his mother. 'You heard what Mrs Davidson said, there isn't much time.'

Back along the corridor, the boy could hear someone howling with laughter. Someone else fighting for breath.

His mother opened the door of the room where his father used to sit and read. The light from the hall found a desk, bookshelves, a chair. Someone was sitting with their back to them. A man who smelled like his father had once smelled. A cotton shirt made ripe by his body and too many cigarettes. His mother went in first and touched the man on the shoulder. He jerked as if he'd been asleep and she calmed him with the same voice she'd used when the boy was small. The man stood up and they embraced one another.

The laughter from the other room rose suddenly as if someone had delivered the punchline to a joke.

A hand moved around his mother's waist and rested on her spine. His mother cried quietly into the man's shoulder and, no longer conscious of the boy standing there, it seemed, confessed all the doubts of her heart and all the longings of her body. But they had fooled her, the laughing people from the village, Mr Davidson and his red dust.

The boy knew that the hand on her back was too small to have been his father's. And he would never have let his nails grow so long.

KRISHAN COUPLAND

THE SEA IN ME

SOMETIMES IN THE bath I plunge my head under the water and will the scars on my neck to open wide like mouths. Nothing. Even if I stay under until my eyes sting and my lungs burn and everything inside me feels like it's about to burst, they stay closed. Perhaps the water's too hot, or too soapy, or maybe even too shallow. Perhaps my brain knows I'm not really swimming.

At the pool it's different. I can drift down to the bottom and sit until my fingers go wrinkly. Only when Mum's not there, of course. When Mum's there I have to train.

What I like most is when I'm the last one at the pool. They switch off the lights and the boys all watch me as they close the pumps and heave in the lane floats. The one who fancies me – his name is Martin – leans on the rolled-up pool cover at the far end and calls to me as I emerge.

'It's almost closing time,' he says.

'One more length,' I say.

And he lets me. He always lets me. Mum would be furious if she knew I wasn't a virgin. She's old fashioned like that. In secondary school she caught me kissing a boy on the field one time and she dragged me off home and yelled about how I was endangering my career. There's no time for boys, what with training and my competition schedule. That's what she says anyway.

Every trophy I've ever won is in the cabinet downstairs. There're other things in there too. Every time we go on holiday Mum buys a shot glass and puts it in the cabinet, and there's a bunch of little ceramic washerwomen as well, all of them grinning and jolly. Mainly it's trophies though, crowded together like a miniature city made of glass and polished wood and gold. She's even kept the stupid paper certificates I got for completing my swimming lessons at school.

When my hair went green I told Mum it was because of all the chlorine, and she wrote me a note for school. I like it. Nobody else has green hair, and it's soft and never gets tangled. When I swim without a cap it floats around my head like a coral reef plant and turns with me, follows me slender and obedient like a tail. I like the way it makes me look: mysterious and strange. And sexy, I think.

Walking me home after a day of school and swimming Martin runs his hands through it, makes a fist of it at the back of my head and pulls. My spine turns hot and liquid. He doesn't say anything, but I know he likes it too.

It's hard to spend time with Martin without Mum knowing. Sometimes I don't do my lengths after school and go to his house instead. When I do that I have to fill his bathroom sink with water and dip my swimsuit in it so that it's not dry when I get home. Mum checks these things.

'You'll thank me later,' she says. She's been saying it for years. Every morning at six she drives me to the leisure centre with the big pool. That early we're almost always the only ones, and I can have the whole pool to practise in. They'll let me in for free sometimes, if they recognise me from the local paper. Every time this happens Mum goes all quiet and pink and smiley, and I hate it.

In the empty water I train with a drag suit. It's like my regular swimsuit but two sizes too big, so that it slows me down and makes me pull harder. Mum stands at the edge watching my turns, watching each perfect lunge through the blueness of the water.

In the changing rooms afterwards Mum stretches me, shakes thick powder into a bottle of water for me. The energy drinks taste like too-thick gravy. I'm cold. I put twenty pence in the hair drier and shiver as the heat rushes over my neck and scalp and shoulders. 'Drink up,' Mum says, and rubs my shoulders till they feel like they're about to fall off.

After school that evening, just before they close the pool, Martin jumps in with me and pins me against the wall under the diving boards. The sheltered, deepest corner. With my back against the wall I can't kick, so it's only him that keeps me floating. Warm bodies in cool water pressed together. Skin feels different under the surface. Most people never find that out.

'Are you going to come and watch me in the semi-finals?' I ask.

'When?' he says.

As well as being a lifeguard Martin wants to own a store some day. He runs a little one at the moment, just selling stuff on eBay. His room is full of it, boxes of clothes piled everywhere in sight. He's always so busy.

'You'll be fine,' he says. 'You're such a good swimmer. You're gorgeous.'

Most of the time I wear a scarf to hide the scars, or

smother them with foundation. For swimming though, it does no good. They only open underwater anyway, and nobody's ever noticed. Mum buys me waterproof foundation. 'Looks are important, love,' she says. 'You've got to win the crowd.'

She doesn't have a clue. I wonder what would happen if I could show the crowd everything. The translucent, froggy webs between my toes and the cascade of beautiful green hair underneath my swimming cap. They wouldn't like it. Would think I was showing off, or that all the success had gone to my head. Nobody can really know what it's like.

Sometimes I have this dream. In the dream I'm in the water swimming, and it's the ocean and I'm not alone. There're all these dark shapes with me cutting through the water. There's hundreds of them, but they all stay just behind my eyes, flitting into murk the second I turn my head.

I'm so happy. I want to live there for ever and ever. Sometimes I wake and I swear I can taste salt, and it takes me a second to realise that what I taste is actually my tears. No way to know why I'm crying. I'm not sad. The dream just makes me feel happy and longing. That's all. It must just be the strangeness of it.

Before the semi-finals I shave my legs. I shave my pubic hair as well. In the bath, with one of Mum's plastic razors, carving away the thick blonde hair. The pale molecules of stubble coat the soapy surface of the bathwater. I wonder if Martin likes that I'm all shaved? Boys like that kind of thing. I've heard them talking.

The skin on the back of my legs is rough. One patch right underneath my backside and another below my knee, both of them silvery and splitting into scale. I get out of the bath and feel myself all over, twisting to see my pale body in the mirror. There's another patch low down on my back as well, the same colour as the surface of an oil spill, rough and warm and slippery.

Mum drives me to the pool an hour early, while everyone's still setting up, and we sit in the cafe. I'm allowed an energy drink, but nothing else. She sips nervously at a watery cup of tea. Sometimes I like feeling this way. It feels like sitting in an aeroplane a moment before takeoff. Today what I mostly feel is tired.

'Remember your turns,' she says. 'They'll be watching you. I'll be watching.'

The stands are full of people. Absolutely full, not just scattered like they normally are. Mum's more nervous than I am. The energy drink has made my stomach feel hot and tight. She lets me have my earphones in for a few minutes while I stretch and warm up, then whips them away. The chlorine smell hits me as I step out of the changing rooms. With echoes and ripples and the pool lights, everything is distorted. This, I think, must be what it's like to live in a bubble on the bottom of the sea.

'And smile,' Mum hisses to me before she disappears.

Minutes later I'm up on the board, a hundred pairs of eyes pressing into me. Can they see the silvery patch of skin on my leg? Is that what all the whispers are?

Noise ripples in here too. The other swimmers like soldiers lining up . . . Some of them look at me when they think I won't notice. I hate this part. I want the buzzer to go so I can dive into the water. Once I'm in the water everything's easy. Once I'm in the water my body knows what to do. If you asked someone how they breathed, asked them the exact way in which they moved their lungs and throat they would be at a loss to tell you. It's the same with me and swimming. It just happens. In the water it'd be harder not to.

I win, of course. I always win. Swimming's easy for me. Mum says I was born swimming, which is true because she had a water birth. That's what she says during every single interview. 'She was born swimming, this one was.' Actually, as it happens, she does most of the talking anyhow. It's best that way. I never know the right thing to say.

The prize is a glass trophy with an etching inside. As we drive home I turn it over and over and, no matter which way I look at it, it's still a dolphin. I like this trophy. It feels proper, like the ocean, like I'm holding a little bit of the sea in my hand. I want to keep it, but when we get home Mum puts it in the cabinet with all the others, and locks the little glass door.

Sometimes I think about telling Mum I don't want to compete any more. I lie on my bed and line up all my words ready like little soldiers in perfect regiments. Ready to run at her words and stick them through with bayonets. It's too easy. It isn't fair. Why can't I ever just swim, without worrying about form or time or turns? I make lists of the reasons and then tear them up and flush them down the toilet so she won't find them when she goes through my room.

It does no good. I don't know how many thousands she has spent on pool fees and swimming lessons and competition entries for me. I don't know how many hundred hours she's put into driving me to and from and training. With all that weight behind me there's no way to stop now.

After school I sit on the bottom of the pool and wait. I don't get cold. I'm never cold in water. My green hair floats up around my head in a big seaweed-coloured cloud, and I watch it. When I'm in water I feel powerful sometimes. I am powerful. I could flick up from the bottom of the pool and swim so fast that nobody could catch me. That's what all the trophies and the medals and certificates at home mean. Nobody can catch me, even if they tried.

I shut my eyes. And then the dream comes up again, rising like silt: I'm swimming in among those dark slivery shapes, and there are thousands of them, so that the water is them and their shadows and the spaces between them and nothing else. In the ocean I can see for miles.

An arm wraps around my stomach and hauls me upward. There's that skin-on-skin underwater feeling and I'm plunged into air, up into air, the last water escaping my lungs in a splutter and cough.

'You're okay?' says Martin. 'You're okay? God, I saw you down there and I didn't know . . .'

I shake myself loose of him. He's still fully dressed, wet through. 'You didn't need to do that,' I say.

Once he's dry we sit on the bench outside, and he offers me a cigarette. I pinch a little bit of the skin of his forearm between my nails. 'Martin,' I say.

'Yeah?'

'Can we go to the seaside?'

After missing the semis he's so anxious to make things up that of course he says yes. And later in his room when he puts his dick inside me it feels right. Doesn't hurt at least, for the first time in ages. It feels like floating in hot water and I want it to go on forever.

I tell Mum that it's a school trip. She wants to know if there's a form but I tell her no since we're only going for half a day. She makes some noises but doesn't ask bad questions. She makes me a packed lunch with sandwiches and Babybel. I leave the house in school uniform and get changed at Martin's house. Martin has a moped. There's only one helmet and he makes me wear it.

'I don't want to,' I say. 'I want to feel the wind.'

When we stop at the services halfway there he lets me take it off and leave it hooked over my arm for the rest of the trip. The wind lifts my green hair and pulls it straight back. I can feel it combing through, strong fingers that trip and fall and rise as I turn my head. We're going so fast. I don't think I've ever moved this fast in the open air before. I can smell the sea miles before we get there. It smells delicious, frothy and thick with life.

We're two of the only people to be seen on the whole wide white beach. A girl is riding a horse out in the surf, and there are men in canoes out on the ocean. Martin leaves his shirt and shoes in the box on the bike and holds my hand all the way down the sand. I want to run, but I'd look silly if I did that. The water when we reach it is dark blue-brown and full of sediment.

'Are you going to swim?' says Martin.

I nod. Of course I'm going to swim. I can't quite wrap my head around it. This is the same ocean that washes up on the shores of America. Huge. This is where life came from, first of all, before there was anything. It looks right. It smells right. I strip down to my bathing suit and wade in. Martin follows, after rolling up the legs of his shorts. He holds both our phones up at his chest, careful not to get them wet.

It's been years since I last swam in the ocean. The memories are there, all faint and faded apart from the smell: that's something I could never forget. I was barely taller than the waves that now lap at my knees. Dad was there, I remember. It must have been very long ago.

When the water's high enough to swim in I lunge down and feel the cold wash of it pass over me and in a second it's not cold any more. My hair slicks back along my body, then floats as I plunge under and kick. I can feel how powerful I am. Powerful. In the swimming pool I was like a tiger in a shipping container, always swiping at metal and empty air.

When I pause and look back Martin is awfully distant. He looks like he wants to follow, but he doesn't know what to do with our things. I wave to him. The waves lift and drop me. I feel like I can breathe clearly for the first time in ages.

When I go under I expect to see them, those shadows from my dream. But there's nothing there. The sediment rushes past like a shoal of tiny fish. I kick deeper. The water feeds into me and I can feel my body elongating, the web between my fingers and toes becoming thicker. I have to go deep, I know. That's where they'll be. I can't hear anything but in the nothing there is sound, I think, some kind of deep and booming voice.

I surface again. I'm further out than I thought, and I know that the things from my dream are further out still. Beyond the bay and further, further. I'd have to swim for days to get there. My body bobs in the current, the water pressing against my chest. I want to go back under. I want to kick through the water and have it hold me.

'I was getting worried there,' says Martin when I return to him. His shorts are wet against his skin.

'You don't need to worry about me,' I say. He kisses me for a while and I wonder if he can taste the things that are different about me. The changedness. The sea in me. 'You look cold,' I say at last. He nods.

'Bloody freezing.'

'You can go back to the beach. I'm going to have one more swim. Out and back, and then we can go. Is that okay? Please.'

He looks at me, halfway puzzled, and I feel very sorry for him. 'Ten minutes,' he says. 'You promise?'

I tell him that I promise, and then watch, waist-deep in saltwater, as he makes his way slowly back to land.

VESNA MAIN

SAFE

IT WAS HER time now. She was safe. She could leave. No one would stop her. She doesn't have to see him again. She knew all that and yet the voice kept repeating the same thing. But something else, not a voice, a force inside her wouldn't let go. That force made her fetch a knife from a drawer in the kitchen. That force made her walk back to the room. That force made her push the blade into Dave, lying sprawled on the floor, snoring. As the steel cut into his chest, he jumped, startled, uttered a cry, of shock or anger - she couldn't tell. Fear ripped his eyes open. He lurched to one side, shaking, trying to grab her, mad from pain. But he was drunk with beer and sleep and she was quicker. She stabbed him again. And then she stabbed Marvin and saw his kind, lined face grimace with pain. And again. And again she had it for Dave. Quick, sharp stabs. In out, faster and faster, like someone going mad chopping onions. Each time she shoved home the knife, his blood spurted its red warmth onto her face, onto her half-naked body, onto the walls around them. It dripped on the carpet; she could feel its drying stickiness on the skin between her toes. Her hand moved as if someone was directing it, pushing it with a long stick as if she were a puppet. And the hand carried on working for a long time after he had stopped making any sound. All she could hear was the swish as the knife passed through his chest. When she stopped, she was gasping for breath. The swish continued. His body lay next to her like a huge wet sponge. The hard work was over. She could relax. She fell backwards into an armchair, her legs stretched out. She had no energy left, her body a rag doll. If he could get up now, she wouldn't be able to fight back. She was certain of that. But he was more dead than the corpses she had seen on the telly. She closed her eyes. She was safe. It was her time now.

She must have dozed off. When she woke up, the blood on her skin had dried. There was daylight and the sun hurt her eyes. Her body shivered with cold. She screamed when she saw him: his eyes bulging like in a horror film. She rushed out of the room. Was he still alive?

She should wash her hands, her body, the carpet, the walls. And him? If he were dead, she could take him somewhere. Hide him. But she wouldn't do any of that. She had killed him. She was going to jail. And then she saw him, a big body stumbling towards her, his eyes bleeding sockets. But the face was kind, the face of Marvin, lined. He was smiling, putting out his hand towards her, checking that her body was warm. Marvin, her mother's friend, who bought her ice-cream, who made sure that she was warm inside and down there. Marvin was kind. But his fingers were cold, bony, an old person's fingers. Not like Dave's, Dave's fingers chubby like sausages. Marvin was kind. Kind to her. Kind to her mother. Why was his face the same as Dave's? She grabbed her coat and ran into the street. She ran, her bare feet slapping the cold tarmac. Dave lumbered after her. She ran until she couldn't see him. But she knew he would come and she was scared.

She banged on the door of a house. She banged and called

until a window opened in a room upstairs. And another one in the neighbouring house. A door unlocked and she rushed in. The rest happened to someone else and she watched it from the side without feeling a thing. People in the house, a police ride, a station, questions – she couldn't tell what they had to do with her – but the questions, so many questions and a doctor who came to examine her for wounds, samples of blood they took and then a shower. She sat on a cracked tiled floor and let the water run over her head, over her hunched body. She saw herself jumping away from Dave as he pulled off her bra and threw it to Nige. She crossed her arms to cover her naked breasts. Nige sniffed her bra. The other man was laughing loudly and banging his fist on his knee. 'Come on, give us a bit of fun,' Dave said, 'a bit more, the last bit.' He tugged at her knickers. Nige had his hand in his trousers and the other man had unzipped himself and was rubbing his cock. Dave pushed her onto the sofa between the two men and then Nige pulled her on top of him. Gavin was next to him. She felt them pull off her knickers. She lashed out, kicking and scratching. It was this or she was nothing. She howled and bit whoever came near. Nige was swearing, mad with pain and anger: 'Fucking bitch, you'll pay for this.' She screamed as he hit her on her face and breasts and forced himself inside her. The other man was holding her legs apart. She went on screaming and scratching and eventually the two men left her alone. 'Can't you shut the bitch up?' Gavin shouted to Dave. 'You need to learn to control your missus,' Nige said. The water became cold but she sat there letting it run over her bare back until someone came and put a towel over her.

They told her he was dead and she neither believed nor disbelieved them. It didn't matter. She was safe. And she wondered whether she had died because everything was different and she was different. She had to be dead. Alive, she had felt that force taking over her and then there were things she loved and things she hated, but now it was all the same. The next day she was in a holding cell when a man came to see her and said he was her lawyer. He was there to help her and he talked and talked. And that same question that the police had asked.

When she had returned from the refuge Dave had been nice, had bought stuff from Iceland and they had tea like a proper couple. He didn't mind when she wanted to see *EastEnders*. He made fun of the story and laughed as he talked about the cleavage of one of the women but that was all right. And then one evening, as she was about to put burgers under the grill, there was a knock on the door and it was Gavin. He had broken down not far from their place and he wanted Dave to help him. She wanted to go with them – she didn't care about missing *EastEnders* – but Dave said she should stay and watch the telly. He said he wouldn't be long. But he was. She was asleep when he returned. She remembered him drunk, pushing himself into her.

'But why didn't you leave?' He didn't listen. Did he want her to repeat it?

The evenings after that followed the same pattern: Dave went out, usually with Gavin and came back drunk. Sometimes, when he was on an afternoon shift, Gavin came over with beer and they would drink before lunch. After Dave had turned up for work drunk for the second time, they sacked him. Of course they did; he was a driver for an off licence and they were strict about such things. Then he started complaining about her not working. She had tried hard, in shops and bars, but there was nothing or else the money was shit – it was better to be on the dole – and every day they argued. He said she should go back on the street but she didn't want to do that any more. He hit her. Once when they quarrelled, the neighbours called the police but all the police did was to tell them to quieten down. That same evening he beat her up so badly that she lost consciousness.

The lawyer interrupted again with that same question: 'Why didn't you leave him?'

She thought for a long time but couldn't think what to say. He was her man, it was proper; it wasn't like Marvin giving money to her mother, it was real, they had dated for real. She wanted to stick with Dave. She could see it wasn't easy for him with no money and no job. She had to help him out. That's what couples did. And he was sorry when he hit her. Sometimes he said so.

'Tits, give us the tits, come on.' That was Nige's voice. And then Gavin echoing him: 'Tits, tits.' She saw herself moving towards the door. But as she turned around, Dave was standing next to her. He took her in his arms and started to dance. It was nice. The men laughed and clapped. Then Dave kissed her and, for a moment, she thought he was thanking her and she would be free to go. She relaxed and let him turn her around, but he surprised her by unclasping her bra. Nige and the other man shouted: 'Yes, tits, get her here.'

'But you could have walked out? You chose not to,' the lawyer said.

It was early afternoon when he came home with Gavin and Nige, carrying six-packs. He pushed her into the bedroom and closed the door: 'Look, help me out. Nige has promised me a job.' He spoke quietly, as if not wanting the others to hear. 'A proper job.' She didn't believe him. He said: 'Nige's brother-in-law is opening a bar and needs a bouncer; I could fix things for him, be around. I have to keep him sweet.' She asked what he wanted her to do. 'A slow dance, and strip a bit . . . put them in good mood . . . that's all.' She stared at him. Three men drinking together and her stripping. That won't be all. She didn't do that any more.

'Look, Tan, you don't want to work.'

'I do. I'll get something. They promised me,' she said.

'Oh, they promised you,' he mocked. 'And you believed them.' He turned away from her, lit a cigarette. 'Have you forgotten Lilla?' he shouted. 'If I had a job, you could look after her, be a proper mum. I'm doing it for both of us.' He sat on the bed, smoking, staring at her. She turned away, looked out of the window. The back yard was paved; that was where they kept the bins and Dave's broken motorbike. She remembered when he tried to repair it and couldn't and made it worse. That was the day when she was cheated and taken to that house. She had agreed to do a job in the car and then there were three men and they had raped her. They didn't even pay and then Dave had hit her when she got home with no money. But it was the motorbike he was really angry about.

The question again, that question she had come to dread. He was thick, this lawyer.

'Tan, come here, babe.' He patted the bed next to him. She didn't trust him, but she obeyed. 'Come on, sit down.' He put his arm around her, kissed her on the cheek and whispered into her ear. 'It's all right, if you don't want to help. But . . . I need work . . . and it's fucking hard to get anything. Nige has promised. I could start next week. That's why I got the beer . . . to celebrate.' He ran the back of his hand across her cheek.

'You get my drift?' He kissed her on the mouth.

'Only stripping, no more?'

'Yeah, of course.'

'Only the shirt and skirt off. I can keep the bra and knickers on, yeah?'

'Yeah, whatever.' He stood up. She wanted to help him but she wasn't going further. She'd do the dance and nothing else. Dave walked out. Through the closed door, she heard him talking to his friends and them laughing loudly.

'Stripping for three drunk men? In your home? That's mad. You were asking for it.' This lawyer was doing her head in. Why was he so stupid? It was only a little strip, nothing else. Helping out.

A few minutes later, one of them shouted: 'Show! When's the show starting?' She heard clapping and cheering. She wanted to tell Dave she was afraid they expected more than a strip. She heard him call: 'Come on, Tan babe, we're waiting.' He wasn't angry.

She opened the door and walked in. Dave had already moved the coffee table to the side and she stepped onto the rug in the middle of the room. Nige and Gavin were slumped on the sofa, beer cans in their hands. Dave sat in the armchair. The stereo was playing. She got on with it straightaway, thinking that the sooner she started, the sooner it would be over. It was important to please Dave by pleasing the men, but she was wary of getting them excited. They leered at her and she hated that. But it would be all over soon. She made herself think it was somebody else stripping, not her. Her mind was on that Great Yarmouth promenade, breeze in her hair, the ice-cream van playing a jingle. Marvin holding her hand. She unbuttoned her shirt slowly, but made sure that her eyes did not meet the men's. With each button she unfastened, the men cheered. Then she took off her shoes, one by one, and the tights – she had she'd had no time to put on stockings – caressing her legs, as if trying to memorise their shape. She moved around, wriggling her hips, dancing barefoot in her skirt and bra. Nige tried to touch her but she managed to move away and he mumbled, 'Teasing bitch.' She went on dancing, but the other man shouted 'Skirt off, skirt off' and she began to tug at the zip, pulling it down and then a little bit up until it was done. She took off the skirt as slowly as she could and then carried on dancing. That was that. No more.

'But even then you could have walked out.' What was he saying?

Gavin pulled her knickers off and forced himself inside her, Nige doing the same from the back. She fought them, biting and scratching, that force inside her giving her strength, incredible strength. They were shouting 'Shut the bitch up' and running out, running away from her.

'Your story's no good. You consented. Why didn't you leave?' the lawyer asked.

Dave was furious, strode towards her, but she was quicker. She locked herself in the bathroom. And then it was quiet. She didn't know how it happened but soon he was asleep. No, she is sure he wasn't dead. She heard him snoring.

'And then? He woke up and attacked you with a knife and you had to defend yourself,' the lawyer said.

No, she was sure that he didn't. He wouldn't have done that. He was a fist man, not a knife man. Besides, he was too drunk and when he fell it was like he had passed out. In a second, he was fast asleep. But she was very angry with him.

Mad at him. That mad like when you think I could kill that person, I could chop them up into tiny bits. But when she went to fetch the knife she wasn't thinking that. She wasn't thinking anything. She was only doing things. No, that's not true. Her body was moving on its own. Her hand grabbed the knife and pushed it inside his chest and out.

The lawyer said that what she had just said didn't sound right and that she was in trouble if she stuck to the story. He said that it didn't happen like that. She was a confused young woman. What did he mean? He was going to write down what happened and she would sign it and then say the same to the police. Why was he asking her then if he knew what had happened? She said it loudly but he didn't answer. Instead, he repeated that she had killed her violent boyfriend in self-defence. He wrote that down into his notebook. But was it Dave or was it Marvin who was dead, Marvin with his kind, lined face? The lawyer stared at her before repeating that it was Dave who had fetched the knife from a kitchen drawer and who had tried to stab her but she had fought him and killed him in self-defence. But what about Marvin? He was checking that she was warm. It was self-defence, she had to remember that. She didn't care either way. She had told him what it was like – she knew, she watched it happen – but if he wanted to believe something else, it was none of her business. She was fine. That force had let go of her. She was safe.

SOPHIE WELLSTOOD

THE FIRST HARD RAIN

SOMEWHERE OVER THE Irish Sea an almighty storm must have exploded, a tempest of such Biblical proportions that a flock of seagulls, a flock of chaotic, tumbling, terrified birds, hundreds upon hundreds of them, had been forced miles inland: herring gulls, black-backed gulls – all now so far away from the wild spray and sleet that Rachael doubted they would ever find their way back to their desolate ocean home.

But what a stupid thing to think. As if seagulls could get lost, or would be bothered by wintery English weather. Rachael knew that the real reason for the God-awful screeching above her was unromantic and mundane: the city's landfill site attracted any number of scavengers, of a variety of species, and the gulls were swooping over hillocks of human waste. Some herrings, at least, would swim safer today.

She gathered her thoughts and concentrated on the scene in front of her. Peter, her ex-husband, and Val, his mother, leaned against the footbridge railings, Peter in a blue anorak over his suit, Val in a too-tight black jacket. They stared north. Val breathed heavily, red-cheeked and rigid-jawed. After a few moments she pulled a green plastic tub from a carrier bag at her ankles. Thirty feet below, the early morning traffic sped by in rhythmic waves, lights still on, occasional windscreen wipers moving like scolding fingers. Rachael had to resist the urge to flick them the V.

Peter took the tub. 'Human ashes are heavier than most people anticipate,' he said. 'They're crushed bone, to be precise, not ash at all. Phosphates and calcium. That's why one mustn't put them on the roses, Ma, no organic value in them at all, none whatsoever.'

As soon as the lid was off, a puff of grey dust blew up and out of the tub, some of it settling on his moustache.

Val looked at her son and opened her hands. Peter tipped a small amount of ashes into his mother's cupped palms. He then nodded at Rachael and she too opened her hands and let him tip a pile of ash into them. She wondered which parts of Terry's crushed skeleton she was cradling. Tibia? Rib? Thick skull?

The lid crunched as Peter screwed it back on. Val tipped some of her ashes back into his hands and then they all became still, waiting for a suitable break in the traffic. At this hour, the M6 was mostly lorries and vans, but with every passing minute the volume of Audis, BMWs and Range Rovers increased as the West Midlands commuters accelerated through the bitter morning.

'We'll just throw ever such a tiny bit,' Val said, mindful of creating a danger to other road users. In these conditions, she'd repeated since leaving the house, in these conditions the safe stopping distance would be at least seventy-five metres, and she would not be held responsible for causing a hazard.

Now, standing by the railings, she looked wildly at Rachael and Peter. 'It was his favourite motorway,' she said, her voice breaking.

They opened their hands and let go. Terry's dust didn't

plummet into the traffic as Val had feared, but was snatched horizontally away from them, whipped into thin cloudy columns which stretched and curled over the hard shoulder towards the junction with the M54. The road to north Wales.

Val whispered something which Rachael could not hear. Drops of moisture collected on Peter's moustache and the seagulls continued their incessant shrieking up above.

After a few minutes of what she hoped was a respectful silence, Rachael put her gloves back on and rested a hand on Val's shoulder.

'Perhaps he's on his way to the caravan,' she said, and instantly wished the words back, heat flooding her face. 'No, no. I'm sorry. I meant—'

Val looked at her in bewilderment. Peter put the plastic tub back in the carrier bag, blinking hard.

Five minutes later the three of them had climbed down the steps and walked to where the Volvo was parked. Rachael sat in the back and let her breath steam up the window. Peter put on Radio 2 and drove at a steady fifty-five miles per hour for fifteen minutes.

The countryside was ugly in this part of the world. Flat, scrubby fields stretched to a horizon jagged with chimneys, tower blocks and steel pylons. Bone-thin ponies stood motionless beside barbed wire fences, and mile after mile of the roadside bramble was strewn with fluttering plastic.

The King's Head Hotel and Executive Golf Club sat five minutes off the dual carriageway, hidden by a shimmering wall of poplar trees. Peter reversed into the first space available after the disabled bays, then got out to open the passenger door for Val and helped her across the car park.

After they'd used the toilets, Rachael bought them all

coffee and carrot cake in the Garden Terrace bar, her treat, she absolutely insisted. They were the only customers.

On a far wall, a widescreen TV showed a twenty-four-hour news channel, the two presenters silently mouthing events unfolding in Libya, Iraq and London, whilst a stream of words slid across the screen.

Rachael said she would stay in the bar whilst Peter and Val took the rest of Terry down to the river, or at least as far as Val was able to walk. After they left, Rachael went to the window and watched the two slow-moving figures with the carrier bag cross the wet lawn. The February drizzle was turning into a cold, hard rain and she did not expect them to be out there for very long.

Two years ago, on a golden September evening, the TV playing impossibly loudly, she had taken Peter's supper plate to the kitchen, put it in the dishwasher and told him she was going for a bit of a walk. He hadn't looked away from the girl dancing with a little white dog.

Peter moved back in with Terry and Val a week later. Rachael kept the house – she had paid for most of it, and Steve moved in after a respectful period. A lazy, workable truce settled between them all and Rachael continued to do Terry's books because she was a good accountant and why not?

She heard a soft chiming from her bag and pulled out her phone. Steve's message was a single question mark. She typed back a single exclamation mark, followed by two x's, then went to the bar and asked for a vodka and slimline tonic. Double.

'Any ice with that?' According to the shiny badge on her

breast, the woman serving was called Lorrelle. She was older than Rachael by about ten years. Rachael shook her head.

'He used to drink here a lot,' Lorrelle said, putting Rachael's glass on a frilly paper mat. Her nails were manicured to a sharp, bloody red. Her lipstick matched.

Rachael flinched. 'You knew him?'

Lorrelle laughed without humour. 'Not personally. But I recognised her, the wife. From the papers. I'm good with faces. Poor cow.' She crossed her arms. 'Sorry. You related?'

'Nope. Daughter-in-law. Ex.' Rachael swallowed the vodka in three long pulls. She wiped her mouth cowboy-style, and slid the glass back to Lorrelle. 'We all make mistakes.'

'Terry Hastings,' Lorrelle said. 'My niece was one of his pupils. Passed first time. Surprise surprise.' Again, the humourless laugh. She waved Rachael's ten pound note away. 'No, you're all right, love.'

Peter and Val returned half an hour later. The cold wind brought with it a swirl of dead leaves which scurried around their ankles like rats. Val's shoes were caked with mud, the tops of her feet spilling out over the tight cream pumps, so wholly and predictably inappropriate for the weather. She sank into the leather sofa, her hair stuck to her cheeks, her chest heaving, her skirt and knees wet through.

She looks like a walrus, Rachael thought, feeling the zip of vodka and caffeine loosen her neck and shoulders. Actually, she looks very, very ill. Days numbered, surely. And then what? Peter would inherit a business that no one would touch with a bargepole and a house with sticky carpets that smelled of dog and bacon.

'So that's that,' Peter said, his eyes hard. He sat back in

his chair, the empty green tub by his feet. He clicked his fingers in the direction of the bar. Rachael watched as Lorrelle slowly turned around. Peter raised his chin and nodded at the cups on the table. Lorrelle stood still, hands on hips. Rachael noticed a small patch of red developing on the side of Peter's neck. He pointed again to the table. Lorrelle cupped a hand behind one ear and raised her eyebrows.

'For Christ's sake,' Peter said, and cleared his throat. 'Refills, if you don't mind.'

Lorrelle didn't move.

'Is there a problem?' Peter said, the red patch spreading up his throat. Rachael wanted to kick her feet with glee.

Lorrelle wiped her hands on a towel and walked slowly towards them, just like a bear, Rachael thought, a bear that had stepped out from its cage.

'What can I get you?' she said, standing over Peter.

'More coffee, thanking you,' Peter said. His neck was puce. 'Ma?'

'I think I'd like a small sherry, please,' Val said. Her eyes were red-rimmed, her cheeks blotchy.

'A sherry,' Lorrelle repeated. 'Fino, Manzanilla, Amontillado, Olorosso?'

Val stared at her.

'Or Harvey's Bristol Cream?'

Val nodded. 'Yes, yes, a Harvey's Bristol Cream. That will be lovely. Thank you.'

Lorrelle looked at Rachael. 'Another mineral water for you?' she asked.

Rachael smiled. 'Thank you. Thank you very much.'

'Perhaps we'll be left in peace now,' Val said. She sipped at the sherry. Peter stared at the ceiling, gripping his coffee, knuckles white. 'Do you want to undo your tie a bit, love?' Val said. 'You know he wouldn't have minded.' Peter shook his head and closed his eyes.

On the TV, the news channel showed a smiling Royal over on the other side of the world shaking hands, dozens of people in native dress dancing energetically around him. Rachael watched as the Royal clapped and laughed, sweating in his suit, trying a few clunky moves himself. A beautiful girl placed a garland of flowers around his neck. Everyone looked so happy, so delighted, so carefree. Rachael imagined herself out there with the dancing natives, the flowers, the sunshine, the awkward Royal. How lovely to be him. How strange and lovely.

'I'll get a cab back,' she said, half an hour later, as Peter and Val stood up to leave. 'I've got nothing on this afternoon. Or I'll call Steve. Really. You go.'

Peter frowned. 'I'll be in touch. About the books. You'll need to tie things up.'

'I know,' Rachael said. 'I do know.'

'Right then,' Peter said. 'Well then. Bye.' He held his hand out.

Rachael took it. 'Bye,' she said. 'Take care.'

Val picked up the empty green tub and put it back in the carrier bag. Rachael kissed her swiftly, then Peter helped her on with her jacket and they headed for the door. A couple of minutes later Rachael heard the Volvo's engine revving, then the crunch of tyres on gravel, and then all was quiet. She returned to the leather sofa.

❧

Lorrelle brought over two large vodkas and two bags of pork scratchings and sat down next to Rachael. They clinked glasses.

'To new friends.'

'New friends.'

Lorrelle opened both packets and tipped the scratchings out onto the table.

'I've got keys to the store room,' she said. 'Perks. Help yourself.' She put a handful of scratchings in her mouth.

Rachael took a couple.

'These'll kill me,' Lorrelle said, crunching, 'but I'm addicted to them. I think it's the salt. I think I'm lacking in salt or something.'

They finished the vodkas and the pork scratchings, then Lorrelle went behind the bar and picked up a pack of Marlboros. Rachael followed her out into the back yard. The rain had stopped and now a pale, wet sunshine picked out silvery drips on the beer crates and barrels.

'How is she?' Rachael asked. She watched a blackbird hopping and pecking around the dustbins; quick, jerky movements: peck, peck, run, peck, peck, run. 'Your niece, how is she now?'

Lorrelle looked up to the sky and Rachael followed her gaze. The seagulls were still there, miles away over the landfill, catching the thermals, rising and dipping crazily in their unknowable world. Lorrelle took a deep drag on her cigarette and then smoke streamed from her mouth and nostrils like a ghost leaving her body. The blackbird, suddenly startled, flew into the shrubbery, calling out a loud *chook chook chook*.

Lorrelle threw her cigarette onto the ground, twisted the stub under her foot and lit another one. She turned to Rachael.

'Kelly? She'll be OK. You know.' Rachael saw tears balancing on her eyelashes. 'She's going to go back to college. She'll be OK.'

FRANÇOISE HARVEY

NEVER THOUGHT HE'D GO

'FELL OFF THE church spire,' said Davi.

'Gravestone landed on him,' said Davitoo.

'Trampled t'death by cows when he cut through the wrong field home,' said Saz.

'Not to death,' said Davi. 'To death means actually dead. He's just a bit bashed up, like.'

Broken arm, three broken ribs, black eye, bust collarbone, top of his foot smashed and plenty of bruises elsewhere, said everyone, though no one could agree how he got it all. Normsmum had her own ideas. She ambushed us outside Missus Lambert's bitshop while we were arguing over how to spend a fiver we'd found. She was fresh off visiting Norm at the hospital. Her eyes were red and puffy like she'd had bees at them, and her make-up was all smeared so her face was difficult to set straight to the eye. We felt bad for her. Felt double-bad because she wasn't far wrong with the direction of her anger, either.

'You all! You there, you bloody lot! I know you had something to do with it. He wouldn't go gallivanting about without you pushing him into it. He could've *died*. I'll pin the lot of you, you mark my words.'

'We didn't do anything, Missus Eames,' said Davi, perfect mix of irritated and innocent. 'We were all home, we all didn't lay a finger on him.' The rest of us nodded and humha-ed.

Normsmum jerked her head back so she was looking at us through slit eyes, down the line of her nose. We must've looked smaller that way – the whole gang'd shot tall over the summer and carried it well, too. She sniffed like she smelt something bad off us. 'Youse all are lying little bastards. Norm'll say what happened when he's up, and then I'll come knocking on every one of your doors. Every. Last. One. And I'll have the hats with me.' She jabbed a finger at each of us, long sharp nail tasting blood and handbag swinging from her fist like she wanted to skip the police and just get stuck in. 'Delinquents, the lot of you.'

We waited a solemn few minutes after she was gone before anyone said anything. It made us uncomfortable to see an adult so close to tears and so close to walloping the shite out of us in one breath.

'Wonder what did happen to him,' said Saz.

'Place is haunted, like we said. Warned him, didn't we?' said Davi.

'I thought that was a joke,' said Davitoo. 'Like, that was the point of the dare. It was a joke.'

'Never thought he'd do it,' I said.

None of us thought he'd do it. We'd known Norm Eames since we were all little kids and he wasn't up to much. Two things you could rely on Norm for: tall tales and bravado like a balloon – puffed round, him, and one push a bit too hard and he'd burst or be away. Or both. We would've liked him more, probably, if he'd admitted to being scared of everything, or when he was hurt or summat. But he never did.

Like, Norm fell off his bike, and told us he wasn't crying, no. He'd hit his head and his eyes were bleeding so he needed to go home.

'You got water for blood?' Davi had said scornfully, and Norm had shouted that Davi didn't know what he was talking about, and he'd kicked his bike and then run for his house.

That sort of thing.

But he kept hanging around us – he was dogged. Always at heel, always eager, and then yapping and running away at the last minute. So you get why we didn't think he'd try for an overnight in the church.

'Not our fault if the gump went through with it,' I said.

'But is it haunted, though? Were we joking about that or not?' said Davitoo, half his fist in his mouth, like he does when he's getting agitated.

'I was joking,' said Saz.

'I wasn't,' said Davi, and he grinned at us all with his teeth only, lips stretched thin, eyes blank. 'Everyone knows it's haunted. There's a graveyard. It's about 500 years old. Fella died in the clock tower, like I said. Haunted.'

We turned and considered the roof of the church, poking up over the top of the bitshop. You could see the whole village from the top of the spire – we knew 'cause we'd seen photos taken by someone who'd gone up there in a hard-hat and hi-viz jacket and not peeped a word about a ghost. She'd gone up in daylight, though, with a guide and a torch, probably. We'd sent Norm up in the dark. But we never thought he'd go, that was the thing. Norm wouldn't sneak out on his mum, not a chance, not without someone pulling him from his room. And none of us had.

❧

'I've had Missus Eames on the phone,' said Mam, as she clattered dishes around fast for dinner. Ran a restaurant, my mam, so she doesn't do food slowly and it's embarrassing having friends over. No such thing as beans on toast round our place. 'In a right state. It's the hypothermia that's made him proper ill, she says, and he was always easily bruised. She says he's in shock and if whoever was with him had taken him to the doctor he wouldn't be in such bad shape.' Mam paused drizzling something sticky over the salad and looked at me sideways from under her lashes – barely a look at all, but you know she's watching. 'She's sure someone must've been with him.'

There wasn't a question mark, quite, but she let the silence hang 'til one grew, and it fair hung off the spire of the church, mocking me through the window. The downside to being able to see the whole village from the church spire was that you could see the church spire from most anywhere in the village. I could see it from my bedroom window, too.

'Weren't nothing with us, Mam,' I said, and chewed more lettuce than I could swallow.

'Kids' games,' she said. 'I'm sure. But if I find out otherwise . . .'

She let that hang, too, and it was worse than the question.

I called Saz. Normsmum had been on at her dad, too, and Saz was spitting fire, locked in her room 'til she told the truth or her dad gave up on it.

'Not even s'posed to have the phone,' she whispered. 'It weren't even us. Davi, wasn't it?'

'You think Davi went out there with him?'

'No,' said Saz. 'I just mean it's always him, pressing the buttons. He always the mouth, don't you notice? But I bet he wouldn't've gone either. Too wimpy. Never thought there'd be anything up there to knock *anyone* around, mind, let alone Norm. You know. *Norm*.' There was admiration in her voice, though, and I thought of the way Norm had looked sideways at Saz when we'd dared him to go to the church, and the red on his face and the sneer on hers. Wondered if it'd all be worth it if he could hear that grudging note.

'Do you think he fell?' I said.

'Cows,' she said. 'He was found on the edge of the graveyard, and that's the cow field. Killer cows. We all know it.'

'Like we know about the ghost,' I said, sharp.

'Sure,' said Saz. She hung up on me.

I went to bed wondering if I could sneak into the hospital and visit Norm without the others spotting me. Or Normsmum, for that matter. Either one would end in a bollocking. I just wanted to check on him, let him know we felt bad for him. Even Mam, who didn't really have much patience for Norm or his mum, figured it was serious. So it was.

I tried to sleep, but it was a bright-moon night and my curtains didn't fall properly shut, so the light slipped through the gap and greyed up my room like an unhappy sun. Eventually I gave up, got up and looked for an old badge or something to pin it shut with. I was pulling the material tight to itself when I looked out into the dark and caught a wink of light over at the church, from the bell tower. Flash and gone. Flash and gone. Flash and hold . . . Like it'd spotted me at the glass and was watching. I fumbled the pin into the curtain and flung myself back under the covers.

In the morning, Mam came into my room looking tired

and gaunt and told me that Norm had died in the night. She held me while I shook and cried. Then she fed me a bit of dry toast and warned me that the hats would be knocking, because now it wasn't just a bashing, was it?

'Trampled *to death*,' said Saz. She tried to put a bit of 'I told you so' into it, but she was sunk as the rest of us. Her lips were dry. Davitoo looked like he would cry any second.

'He were younger than me,' he said, like this was new information.

'Younger than all of us,' said Davi. 'The ghost doesn't care about *age*.'

'Shut up about that bloody ghost,' said Saz. 'It's not funny now.'

'It was never a joke,' said Davi.

'My mam said it was hypothermia that did for him,' I said, wanting to get the conversation away from ages and ghosts. 'If he'd been left somewhere warm, he would've been OK.'

'Like he would've landed in a warm bath after he fell from that height?' scoffed Davi.

'Fuck you,' said Davitoo, shocking us all to silence. 'He was younger than us, and we sent him up that there, in the dark, on his own. Don't none of you feel bad at all?' He glared at us, and then the glare crumpled, and he turned away, shoulders hunched. Dropped his crisp wrapper in the bin and walked off without looking back.

'Touchy,' said Davi.

'He's right,' said Saz.

I nodded.

We fell silent again as Normsmum hobbled past. She had a couple of other women with her, holding her up it looked like. Couldn't even tell you where she'd been or where she was going, but as they drew level with us she stopped, and her entourage stopped with her, and they all stood, swaying slightly. We shrank back into the shadow of the bitshop, waiting for the blows to land, or the words.

She raised her head with effort and looked at us. Her face had collapsed in on itself with grief, like she'd been crying so hard she'd swallowed her teeth and her eyes had fallen back in her face. Her stare was unfocussed, but it held us all the same. After a long while, one of the women gently squeezed her shoulders, murmured something in her ear. The group of them shuddered back into motion, shuffled off down the street. Normal time and normal sounds returned.

'I'm away home, lads,' said Davi, blinking like he'd just woken up. He dropped his crisps and fair ran off down the alley.

Saz sighed and crumpled what was left of her crisps in her hand.

'There was a light,' I said.

'Yeah, I saw,' she said.

'I was going to visit him today.'

'Me too,' she said.

'What do you think really happened?' I asked.

'Killer cows,' she said, firmly. And then she took a deep breath like the next words would cost her. 'Or that bastard Davi, playing ghost.'

'We wouldn't do anything like that,' I said, sure of it.

'Sure *we* wouldn't,' she said.

She went home and I threw up, suddenly, on the side of the bin, and Missus Lambert came out of the shop and shouted at me.

❧

I couldn't sleep for watching out for that light, and watching out for the hats, and wondering what the payback is for the person who didn't do anything, really, but didn't do the right thing, either. Like, probably hundreds of times.

The funeral was a Friday and it was the last week of the holiday. The overriding feeling at the crematorium was resentment that Norm hadn't had the decency to wait another few days. The whole class turned up, of course, and even though Davitoo was still not talking to us, and even though Saz couldn't look at Davi without flinching, we flocked at the back of the crowd out of habit, carefully out of the way of Normsmum's roving, vacant stare. The Eameses were regular church-goers, they had a family spot and everything, but it would've been bad taste, we supposed, to bury Norm in the graveyard where he'd been found.

'Vicar's proper upset,' whispered Saz to me, as we waited for the service to start. Nerves had her running her mouth off. 'Says it's hard enough getting people through the door as it is.'

'Shut up,' said Davitoo. 'They're starting.'

It was excruciating, the whole thing. Who knew that so many people had nice things to say about Norm Eames? Davitoo cried during the singing, and Davi looked like he wanted to smack him upside the head for it. Saz whispered to herself the whole time, so quiet that I'd no clue what she was saying. I counted every freckle on the back of my own hands. When we filed outside, nearly the first ones out, we stood awkwardly for a second, trying not to look in the direction of the church.

'It's done, then,' said Davi.

'What is?' snapped Saz, and if her voice had teeth there would've been blood.

Davi looked at her like it was a stupid question. 'Well, that's it, isn't it? He's gone. Hats have been and gone. End of the matter.'

'Have you not seen the light?' said Davitoo, sounding faintly ridiculous, like an old-time preacher.

'Fecking what light?' said Davi, and he said it so viciously that we knew he had. His eyes were nearly as red with anger as Davitoo's were with sorrow. 'The ghost light? I told you.'

'It's not. A bloody. Ghost.' Saz got right up in his face. And then more people poured out the crematorium, so we all took a breath and a step away.

'Prove it,' said Davi, and Davitoo groaned. He kicked the dirt and walked away without looking at anyone of us. And then we were three and, just like last time, we agreed we were meeting Saturday midnight, at the edge of the graveyard.

Just like last time, I lay in bed and twitched the minutes away. I tried not to think what would happen if there was a ghost, or if Mam woke up and saw my bed empty, or if Mam didn't wake up and there wasn't a ghost and how stupid would we feel. This time, though, I couldn't shake that maybe there hadn't been a ghost before, but there would be one now, and it'd be Norm and by Christ would he have it in for us.

Just like last time, come 11.15, I could hear Mam's whistling snore starting up at the other end of the house. Come 11.30 my feet and hands had gone numb and cold with fear and I didn't fancy I could pull myself out of bed even if I wanted to. Come 11.45, I should've been dressed and gone. I sat on the edge of the bed with one sock on and my jumper over my head and shivered. Norm's ghost, in the bell tower. Norm's ghost, drifting through the graveyard. Norm's ghost, crying tears of blood and wielding all the power that ghosts get when they've come to avenge their deaths.

Come midnight, I sat at my bedroom window, not daring to touch the curtains, but staring through the gap. The moon had thinned, so the village was less lit than the night before and the church was a shadow – but I watched just the same for Saz and Davi and the light, which came again. Flash and gone. Flash and gone. Flash and on on on. I fancied I saw a face behind it. I fancied I saw them through the church walls, climbing up what were surely rickety and dusty steps. I fancied a scream cutting the air, but it was the owl in the oak two doors over, and the wind besides.

None of this was like last time. Last time I'd slept the night through with the relief of a coward in a good hiding place.

Mam answered the door to the hats while I was brushing my teeth through my yawns. She called me down and I came, stupid, in my idiot childish pyjamas and my purple toothbrush still in one hand, and I knew straight off, or thought I did. There were two of them, both women, and both of them looking too sympathetic for it to be good news or suspicion.

'There's been an accident, love,' said Mam, just like she had when she'd got the call about Norm. 'They've got some questions.'

Not Saz, not Davi. Or maybe Davi, but please, god, not Saz.

'Were you out with David Tunnall last night?' said one of the hats – I couldn't tell them apart through their uniforms.

And then I don't know how I answered, because I tried to

tell them there was no way, *no way* Davitoo would've been out last night. He wasn't speaking to any of us, I think I said. He walked away, I think I said. And we said we'd go, but I didn't go, and none of us did that time or likely this time, and I didn't go anyway and and and. Panic took my words and rushed them through without any of my mind taking part. I know I asked if he was OK. And they said, I think they said, they said: 'He's very ill. He's in hospital. We're trying to find what happened.'

I asked if I could see him.

They said family only.

And then Mam held me while I shook and cried. I didn't go out to our place at Missus Lambert's bitshop where the others would be. We'd be pitied, I knew. And we'd be looking at each other like Normsmum had looked at us. The loss of *us*, with Davitoo lying up in the hospital, was more than I could face. But I knew; everyone knew: broken wrist, broken jaw, two broken ribs, black eye, broken nose, punctured lung, ankle smashed and plenty of bruises elsewhere. Left cracked and freezing at the edge of the graveyard and no one could agree on how.

I sat in the garden, my back to the church, and stared at the clear horizon down the hill. No ghosts, that way. No spire, no bell tower, no Norm. Just hills down to fields and the river rolling by. I heard the doorbell jangle and Mam murmur low and send away whoever it was. We passed a quiet weekend. Mam made beans on toast for Sunday, and let me watch shite TV. And on Monday morning, she grit her teeth at me in sympathy and packed me back to school with the rest, all the same.

We ran into each just outside the school gate, like we'd

planned it for a stage show. I sort of wish we *had*, just for the sake of the rubbernecks and stickybeaks who fell quiet when they saw us. We could've put something good together. A showdown. The grand finale. But instead we slowed and fell quiet as well and the space between us and the gap where Davitoo should be pulsed and pained 'til Saz spoke.

'I didn't go,' she said. 'My Da locked me in.' I hugged my relief to myself.

'I didn't go,' said Davi, with twist to his lips. 'Of course I didn't. It's haunted, like we said.' Saz looked like she'd lamp him and took half a step, but he stared her down. 'Killer cows?' he spat on the ground between them. 'I told you.' He didn't even smile this time. He'd got skinnier, toothier in the past week. His eyes had gone dark. 'I told you all it was up there.'

We left him outside the gates and went to face the whispering mob.

That night the light at the church went flash and gone. Flash and gone. Flash and gone. Flash and on. And on.

PETER BRADSHAW

REUNION

SO I'M SITTING here in the hotel foyer on one of the big squashy sofas. I've checked out, paid the bill and my wheelie suitcase has the extendable handle up, ready to go. But the guy on reception says the taxi's going to be another quarter of an hour. This gives me a bit of time to think. And after the events of the last twenty-four hours I've been trying to work something out.

I've been in love three times during my life. Once was when I was married in my forties. That was with Sally. We were having an affair, although neither of us said that word out loud. Once before that, was in my early thirties, with Michiko, now my ex-wife. And once when I was just eleven years old, with Lucy Venables, the girl who lived next door. She was also eleven.

I'll quickly tell you about the breakup in each case.

Easily the most painful was with Sally. I'd scheduled one of the covert semi-regular dinner dates that often led to something back at her apartment. I'd been a little bit early, sitting at a table, working up the courage to make some sort of declaration to her, trying to think what I might say, when she turned up and started saying to me – even before she'd sat down – that she had fallen in love with somebody else, and they were moving in together.

I numbly nodded my absolute and immediate acceptance of this situation. I even did this lip-biting little smile, taking it well, you see, like a reality TV contestant getting told he's not going through to the next round. Sally said that under the circumstances, it was probably better if we put dinner off until some other time, having not actually removed her coat. She had never looked more beautiful, more strong and free.

With Michiko, it was some time after that in Tokyo. We had gone there for her mother's funeral. After the ceremony, back at the family home, we sat silently on a black leather couch with ice-cold aluminium armrests. Michiko just asked me, really quietly, where I would be living when we got back to London.

And as for the last case, well, there was no break-up as such, but my eleven-year-old's passion for eleven-year-old Lucy Venables was just as real as my other loves. I've found myself thinking of Lucy Venables ever since I arrived here at the hotel for this conference for people like me involved in the pharmaceutical industry.

Last night there was a drinks reception. We had these name-tags, Mine was written in biro, 'Mr Chatwin'. Waiters circulated with drinks. The canapes were meagre. I got quite drunk, and after a while I fancied a cigarette, so I went out through a sliding door onto this large artificial lawn they have, starkly lit with security lights, like a cross between a golf course and a football pitch.

There was a woman on the grass, smoking, with her back to me. I got this really strange feeling and headed across the astroturf towards her, with a half-formed idea about asking for a light. My strange feeling got stranger the nearer I got.

Was it . . . ? Could it actually be . . . ? There was nothing else for it. I was going to have to talk to her.

'Excuse me,' I said. 'I wonder if you . . .'

She turned to face me, and immediately gaped in dawning recognition. Her name tag read: 'Dr Venables'. She actually pointed at my 'Mr Chatwin' tag with the non-smoking hand which she then clapped over her mouth.

'Elliot! Oh my God! Oh my God! Is it you? Elliot!'

'Hi, hello,' I said, not knowing what else to say.

'Oh my God! Elliot! This is so weird! I was thinking about you this afternoon! Just now! So weird! I was thinking of that time in our back garden! With the darts! And Dad hitting you! Oh my God! And we never got a chance to talk to you or say sorry or anything!'

She was clearly drunker than me. I didn't know what to say, so I just smiled.

'Do you remember *me*, Elliot?' she asked.

'Of course,' I replied.

'And all that with my dad . . . and the darts . . . I'm so sorry! Gosh, do you know for years after that I used to think about you.'

'Oh, I really don't remember too much about it . . .' I then said airily.

That of course was a lie. The whole story came back into my mind, in every detail, with immense clarity and force. Lucy Venables's family had moved into the house next to mine at the beginning of the baking summer of 1976. I was an only child with few friends. One endless hot day, I was riding my bicycle round and round on the flagstones of my front yard.

Eventually, I fell over and heard someone giggling. I turned around to see Lucy staring at me.

'You're not very good at that, are you?' she said pertly.

I couldn't think how to reply. Then she said: 'Why don't you come in, for some lemonade?'

We went through Lucy's front door, through their hall and into the back kitchen. Lucy poured out two glasses of Corona lemonade from a stippled bottle taken from the fridge and we went out into the garden. Then we sort of played in her Wendy House for a bit until her mum came out into the garden with Lucy's little sister.

'Hello!' she said brightly. 'You must be Elliot. I had a nice chat with your mum yesterday, Elliot. We have to go now. Lovely that you've made friends with Lucy. Bye!'

We played a bit more in the Wendy House. Soon it was time for me to go.

Every day this scene would repeat itself. Without ever arranging it in advance, I would hang around outside the house and Lucy would come out and invite me in to play in her garden. We would play doctors and nurses. Silly baby stuff, considering that we were eleven-year-olds.

Soon I was deeply in love with Lucy. There is no other way to describe it. And it was more poignant and intense for the lack of any sexual feeling. Just a hot, sick feeling in my tummy. And when Lucy would start to make fun of me and be cross with me, the feeling was even worse.

It all came to a head one Saturday afternoon. Lucy and I were listlessly playing and little Chloë would try to join in, but she was sharply dismissed: 'Go *away*, Chloë!' She hung back, talking sadly to her doll. I was hot and bad-tempered and finally Lucy asked me what the matter was.

'May I give you a kiss?' I asked.

Lucy was silent, and I stared down at the ground, astonished at my own boldness, but smugly conscious of having turned the tables. Suddenly, Lucy said to Chloë: 'Come here!'

Obediently, she followed as Lucy led her over to their shed, whose door had a dartboard and three darts. She plucked out the darts, stood Chloë up against it and, taking a box of coloured chalks from somewhere, proceeded to draw a loose outline around the little girl's head and shoulders, about twelve inches clear. Then Lucy offered the darts to me.

'There. If you can throw all three darts so they stick in the door, inside the line, but without hitting Chloë, then I'll kiss you.'

Saucer-eyed Chloë stayed perfectly still against the shed door, clutching her little doll.

'OK,' I said, taking the darts and positioning myself about seven feet away. I sized up my first throw, the dart-point lined up at eye-level, rocking back and forth on the balls of my feet. Then I threw.

The dart landed just above Chloë's head.

'Well done,' said Lucy coolly. 'One down, two to go.'

I cleared my throat. After a few more little feints, I threw the second dart.

This one landed just to the left of Chloë's neck, inside the line. That counted. But now her lower lip was trembling; her eyes brimmed and she was starting to shift alarmingly about.

'Stay still, Chloë!' ordered Lucy. 'All right, Elliot. Third and last dart. Get this right, and it'll be a very big kiss for you.'

My hand trembled. I wobbled my arm freely from the shoulder, to loosen it up, jogging briefly on the spot.

Then I raised it and prepared again. I threw. A clumsy one – in the direction of Chloë's left eye. She flinched, turned; and it went into her ear. Chloë put her hand up to it; a trickle of blood ran down her forearm.

I panicked. I ran up and pulled the dart out of her ear. She screamed. And Lucy's father ran out into the garden. My little victim ran up to him and hugged him around the waist, sobbing desperately.

'What the bloody hell's going on here?' he thundered.

'Elliot was playing a sort of William Tell game daddy,' said Lucy with a sweet smirk.

Her father walked up and smacked me once across the face. Then he stood aside as I blubberingly ran out through the kitchen and back to my house. I never dared tell my own parents what had happened and soon after that, Lucy's family moved away and I never saw her again.

It all came back to me with this very attractive woman in front of me.

'Daddy used to talk about you a lot over supper,' she said. 'I think he knew he shouldn't have hit you.'

'Oh, I really can't remember,' I replied.

We were standing flirtatiously close.

'I don't think you ever got that kiss, did you?' she said.

'No,' I said Elliot. 'Well, I wasn't entitled to it.'

'This party is very boring,' she said.

'Yes.'

'Why don't you come up to my room and I'll give you a kiss now.'

She turned on her heel and went back through the party and into the foyer. I followed.

We got into the lift, in which we were alone. We kissed.

Once at the sixth floor, we got out and headed for her room three doors along. Once inside, we kissed again, rolling on the big double-bed. I began clawing her clothes off and, panting, she plucked at my belt.

'Oh Elliot!' she gasped. 'Call me by my name. Say my name.'

At that moment I swept up her hair, to kiss her neck, and this revealed her ear, cut and disfigured by my dart. In the next instant, I complied with her request:

'Chloë . . .'

I left her room some time after that. She checked out early this morning before I was up.

Ah. The man on reception says my taxi's going to take a while yet and he wants to know if I'd like a complimentary drink from the bar.

I think I shall ask for a Corona lemonade.

LAURA POCOCK

THE DARK INSTRUMENTS

THEY ARE NEATLY laid out on the workbench in size order, starting with the smallest on the left. That's important. Keeping your tools handy is one thing. But when you reach for a heavy-duty, skew chisel knife, that's what you want to pick up. Details matter.

Unfortunately, some nights you can never be sure that you've returned everything to its proper place. Even if you remember arranging everything precisely - even if you *distinctly* remember checking and rechecking - sometimes doubt lies next to your head on the pillow and whispers in your ear that you are wrong. That something's out of place.

So you get up.

You walk across the bare floorboards, dragging your calloused feet through the dust. The key to the garage is hung up in its usual spot by the door - you take this as a good sign that everything's five-by-five. But you still need to check just in case.

Just in case. The phrase you use so often now that hearing it has become as commonplace as the sound of your own name. Unplug the electric heater, just in case. Lock the window, just in case. You never finish the sentence or conceive the consequence of inaction: just in case *what*, exactly, never comes up.

There is a chill in the air tonight but you don't mind. It barely registers. You concentrate on the task: you fumble the key into the lock with a shaking hand and slide the garage door up. The smell hits you immediately.

You pretend to ignore what's under the white tarpaulin on the table in the middle of the garage. You walk around it, as though the peaks and troughs in the tarp don't inspire any fascination. Out of the corner of your eye, you see it move, but you pretend you don't. And there, resting on a green towel in size order, are your knives.

They wink up at you from a square of moonlight let in by the window, but when you run your fingers down each tool, your hand casts a long shadow across the blades. Your fingers walk along the white beech wood handles and the ergonomic tactility pleases you. Little beauties. Everything is just as it should be.

When you turn around to go back to the house, you see it again. The tarpaulin. You hold your breath and you allow your greedy eyes to take in the entire table. You reach out to touch it. You'd known all along that walking past and pretending to ignore it a second time was out of the question.

This is the real reason you got out of bed. A small part of you knows that. The knives were just an excuse. A cold breeze rustles the tarp and it moves like before. Now that you're here anyway, you tell yourself you might as well have a little look. Make sure everything's A-OK. You take a fistful of the tarp and are just about to whip it off, when a light flashes in your eyes.

'Who's there?' whispers the light-bearer.

You drop the tarp. In the white beam of the flashlight, you feel caught. Your instinct is to put your hands in the air, but you know this will imply guilt and you quickly let your arms fall to your sides.

'Oh hell, Marshall! You about gave me a god-damned heart attack!' you cry. This is good. You deflect blame.

'Sorry, Bobby!'

You sigh. No one else has called you Bobby since you were a teenager. Marshall had never adjusted to calling you Robert. This isn't the time to correct him.

'I heard a noise out here. I saw your garage door was open so I assumed the worst,' says Marshall.

'Would you get that light out of my eyes?' You pat your chest with your right hand.

'Sure, sure.' He points the flashlight downward and now you can see his wide eyes. 'What are you doing out here? It's past two in the morning.' The eyes move around the garage, searching for answers before finally landing on your face.

You think. You have known Marshall since you were both kids, but you were always in the smart class. You can talk your way out of this. Your mind shuffles a deck of possible answers and finally lands on the sympathy card. You can't play this card often. If you do, it stops working. But this is an emergency.

'Ah, well, it's my knee again. I've been trying to get organised out here and a few days ago I knelt down to move some of those paint cans. It's been keeping me awake since.'

'Can't they do anything for that knee? With you being a decorated war hero and all, you'd think that—'

You let him talk. You've heard this speech before. He's just getting to the part where he calls it a travesty and you begin to wonder what his reaction would be if you told him the truth. Your mouth is now full of the sentence you could say. You could tell him what the doctors have told you: that there is no pain.

There's no physical reason for the pain you're experiencing, Mr McNeil. It has healed well for a gun-shot wound, barely any scar-tissue. You've been to three doctors and they've all confirmed it. What would Marshall make of that? You test the water with:

'They don't really know what's wrong with it.'

But this just invigorates his rant about what this country is coming to. No, Marshall is the wrong person to talk to about this, and you have allowed him to dictate the line of conversation too long. You remember where you are. Marshall's proximity to your secret. There's a tightness in your chest and you realise it's been there since the moment he shone the damned flashlight at you. He needs cutting off.

'So anyway, sorry to have woken you, Marshall. I couldn't sleep. I thought I might have left the heater on out here, so I got up to check.'

'You oughta be careful, walking around in the dark,' says Marshall. He grips his dressing gown tight in the centre to save his chest from the cold air. 'You don't want to make that knee worse.'

'No, not at all,' you agree. 'Well, it's getting late, so . . .'

But you can tell he's not fully listening. He has finally seen the table, and is walking towards it.

'Whoa – what's all this?'

You sigh.

'It's just a project I've been working on.' You don't like where this is going but once the cow is already dead, you may as well eat the steak. 'Would you like to see?'

'Would I ever!' He points the torch back in your face, and you are smiling now.

'All right, Marshall. Just do me one favour first: pull the garage door closed behind you. We wouldn't want to expose what's under here to the wind.'

'Good idea.'

You watch him slide the garage door to the ground. He does it slowly, quietly, like you should have on your way in. You click your tongue and give him a nod.

'Attaboy.' He never seems to mind that you speak down to him. If anything, you sense that he likes it, which is odd for a guy in his thirties.

If you had known twenty minutes ago that you'd be about to do this, you'd have stayed on the couch, counting the ceiling slats. But you're here now, and it can't be helped. You tell Marshall to take two corners of the tarp and gently lift before moving it to the side of the table, so as not to disturb what's underneath. Wouldn't want to spoil the impact.

Together, you lift the tarp like unmaking a bed, and the objects below are revealed. You suddenly feel vulnerable.

Marshall gasps.

'Oh, my...' He stands with his hands pressed together in front of his chest. He seems to instinctively know you don't want him to touch. He knows these are yours.

You watch him as he looks at the miniature model town you've created with your hands. The model buildings and trees stand proud in the beam of Marshall's torch. *Look at us,* they seem to say. *Aren't we special?*

'Bobby! I had no idea. I knew you were talented in shop class when we were kids. I've always loved those chess sets you make . . . but this is something else!'

You say nothing. You just watch him and tell yourself you can show him the town without revealing its secret. Your secret.

'This is Woodbury, isn't it?' he asks, but he doesn't take his eyes off the miniature town to see me nod. 'Oh, wow! It's all here. You got Main Street all perfect: Barney's Hock Shop, the pancake house, Chick's Hardware Store.' He shakes his head in what seems like awe.

You can't quite be sure, but you think that the feeling in your chest is pride. You figure this is how new parents must feel when they are told their babies are beautiful.

Marshall walks a few steps around the table. When his hand brushes against a rough indentation, he shines the torch to reveal a compass carved into the surface. He chuckles and shakes his head again.

He moves north of Main Street to Little Hill. The model of All Saints Evangelical Church is nestled into the side of the hill, just as it is in the real Woodbury.

'Would you get a load of this?' He claps you hard on the back. 'Kristy and me, we got married in this church.'

You say nothing. The truth is, Marshall's wedding is one of those memories that are now so hazy, so tarnished by the fact that the following week you shipped out and your life went to hell. But you don't mention that. Instead you try to bury the thought by staring at your handiwork.

'Best day of my life,' he continues. 'Before Little Jim was born, anyway. Hey – you even got the missing stained-glass window.' He looks at you in confusion. You panic. Could Marshall figure you out? 'But why would you include that? It wasn't exactly a great moment for the town, to hear that vandals had broken it.'

Your heart feels like mortar rounds firing in your chest.

'It's a coincidence, that's all. I'm still working on the church. Stained glass is no simple thing in miniature, you know.'

Good. This is good. Marshall is nodding and his attention is caught by the next tiny treasure. You watch in dismay as he reaches out to touch the yellow school bus in front of Woodbury Elementary. You had thought there was an unspoken understanding of no touching, but apparently not. Your stomach lurches as he turns the bus upside down and spins the rear left wheel with an index finger. He giggles like a kid and sets the bus back down.

'This is unbelievable, Bobby. I always wondered what you were up to in here. How long did it take you?'

'I don't know, it's just a hobby.' You shrug and give him your best *Aw, shucks* smile. A hobby. It had started out so innocently.

'A hobby that could earn you some proper moolah, friend. You should start a website. "Tinkertowns.com" has a nice *cha ching* to it, wouldn't you say?'

'Ha!' You try to say very little. Your palms are sweating. You realise now that you just want him gone.

Marshall moves west, toward the houses.

'You even got our street. Kristy would love this.' He bends down to look at the model of his own house, 1360 Rovello Drive. 'These are so realistic, I feel like I could look through Randy's window and see his *X-Men* posters.' He shakes his head, then stands up straight. 'Have you ever put lights in these houses? You could make bespoke Christmas villages.'

You clench your fists. You tell him that wouldn't be a good idea. It's not safe.

'So you've tried it?'

You try to appear calm. You say yes.

'So what happened?'

You tell him it had started a fire. Your eyes flit briefly to the shelf where the burnt model house stands. You blink a few times to try to cover yourself, but Marshall is already walking to the shelf and has no reservation about taking the charred building down.

'I see now. You're right, this could have been nasty.' He turns it in his hands and places it back on the shelf. When Marshall moves back to the table, you think you've gotten away with it.

'Listen, Marshall, I'm beat. I think we should get back to our beds, what do you say?' You think you're speaking normally under the circumstances.

'Well, I could just about look at this thing all night, but I guess you're right.'

You want to let out a sigh of relief but you know it would be a huge tell to let slip on the final hand. Marshall helps you cover the town with the tarp, and you even manage to crack a joke about 'tucking her in'. When you're out of the garage and the door is locked tight, you think you are safe.

Then he turns to you.

'Wait.' He frowns. He is whispering now that you are back outside. 'That burnt house. It was the Henry place, right?' He takes a few steps to the right and leans to look in the direction of Phillip Henry's newly restored house.

You freeze up. You would open your mouth to answer, but he's already connecting the dots in his head.

'Uh huh,' he says, and scratches his rough chin. The noise of it sounds like sandpaper. 'It was definitely the Henry place. How strange.'

'Strange? How so?' Your acting skills have been worn precariously thin tonight. You wish you'd just stayed put on the couch earlier. You wish you'd never started building the town. More than anything, you wish you could just tell Marshall to mind his damned bees wax.

'Well, yeah . . . what with the real fire in the Henry place last year,' he said. 'What a coincidence!'

You watch a frown form as his gaze shifts from the new Henry house across the street to the black remains of the model on the garage shelf. Marshall then looks at the dark outline of the tarp for several seconds before his widened eyes fall on you.

Perhaps it is just your heightened nerves, but you could swear he looks paler now. He backs away from you a step. Apparently, Marshall has a lousy poker face.

'You had better go inside, now,' you say. 'It's dangerously cold.'

He tugs his robe closed and treads lightly toward his home. You watch him hurry inside. Marshall's door shuts with a click. You stand in the crisp November night for a further five minutes to check he doesn't come back out.

Just in case.

IRENOSEN OKOJIE

FILAMO

THE LAST MONK told the tongue that holding a naked sheep's head underwater would undo it all. Some time before that, prior to the madness beginning, old Barking Abbey loomed in the chasm, grey, weather worn, remote. Inside the Abbey, a tongue sat in the golden snuff box on an empty long dining table: pink, scarred and curled into a ruffled, silken square of night. The previous week, the tongue had been used as a bookmark in a marked, leather-bound King James Bible, page 45 where the silhouette of a girl had been cut out, loaded with words like high, hog, clitoris, iodine, cake, its moist tip glistening in temporary confinement. The week before that, the tongue had been left in the fountain at the back of the Abbey, between winking coins. There, it pressed its tip to a stray ripple, cold and malleable, shaping it into a weight, pulling it down, under, up again. Several weeks back, it had been in a hallway window, leaning into Mary's hands, whose fingertips tasted of a charred, foreign footprint from the grass. Her fingertips had sensed a change in the air before the monks came, when the corridors were quiet, expectant. Molecules had shifted in preparation for a delivery. The monks arrived through a hole in time on a cold, misty morning, transported via a warp in space that mangled the frequencies of past and present. They arrived curling hands that did not belong to them. Unaware that this would have consequences none foresaw, except a tongue bending in the background, unaware of the repercussions of time travel.

Each time the tongue was moved, it lost a sentence. The monks missed this in their ritual of silence. They had done for weeks, walking around rooms with arms behind their backs, bodies shrouded in heavy brown robes, shaven, sunken heads soft to the touch. They trod this new ground carrying yolks in their mouths, hardening as morning became noon, noon became evening, and evening became night.

One morning, the monks found a miller's wife gutted on the stone wall enclosing the allotment, a white felt cap shoved into her mouth, her husband's initials embroidered in blue at the top right corner of her bloody apron: V.O. They threw salt on her skin. The tongue tasted the sharpness, and that night, Dom Vitelli made the noise of a kettle boiling in his sleep. He began to tremble covered in a cold sweat. He fell to the floor, stuck.

The next morning, the monks rose to discover the empty well near the stone outbuilding surrounded by plump, purple jabuticaba fruit, tender and bruised, the colour dwindling in areas as though a god was sucking it through a crack in the sky. Lonely figures in their heavy brown robes, the monks held their hands out as they circled the abbey. They heard the sounds of buses on the high street, car doors slammed shut, trains grinding to a halt. They caught items that fell through noise, things they had never seen: a white adapter plug from the sound of a plane speeding through the sky, a black dog muzzle Dom Oman later took to wearing when sitting by the fountain, a knuckle duster that fell from the sound of a baby crying. They placed these items at the altar in the chapel, flanked by candles on either side whose blue flames bent, then shrank sporadically. They took turns holding their palms over the flames. By the time the monks began their chores, the cockerel that had fallen over the walls from a car horn began to smash its beak into a jabuticaba fruit. Afterwards, it jumped into the stream connected to the Roding River, following a thinning, yellow light it attempted to chase into the next day.

The tongue was warm in Filamo's pocket, pressed against a copper coin bearing the number two in Roman lettering. The musty taste of old items passing through lingered. Filamo, a cloaked figure, a betrayer amongst the monks, stood outside the prayer room, fingering a swelling on the tongue, listening quietly. Dom Emmanuel paced inside, the only other place speaking was permitted aside from supper during this imposed period of silence. A slightly forlorn figure, he shook. The bald patch on his head looked soft like a newborn's. Light streamed through the stained glass window where three naked cherubs wore angry, adult expressions and had changed positions again overnight. One lay on its side holding an ear, the other was eating stigmata injuries and the third at the bottom-left corner had tears running down its cheeks into the jabuticaba fruit growing through its chest. Dom Emmanuel faced the silence of the cross on the nave wall without the figure of Christ, which had turned up at supper two days before, bleeding between slices of bread. There were three deep, wooden pews behind the Dom, half-heartedly built, scratched on the seating. Dom Emmanuel began to walk back and forth. Then, he paused momentarily as though to catch his breath, chest rising and falling. He held his arms out, confessing that lately he had begun to worry about his lover withering in a wormhole. The man Dom Emmanuel loved had not made it through this time, stuck in a winter that would quickly ice his organs and distribute the seven languages he spoke into the orbit for other monks to grab and stow away along with new disguises.

Dom Emmanuel could feel that cold in his bones, an absence of language, lightness in his tongue. Recently, Dom Emmanuel had dreamt of them running through lush, sunlit fields naked, penises limp at first, then turgid, moist at the tips, till thick spurts of sperm dribbled and their irises glinted. He missed the warmth of holding another body skin to skin, the innocence of early youth, the freedom of making mistakes. He moaned that his hands ached; that they had begun to talk to him, consumed by restlessness, till he sat up in bed sweating, tense, listening to a distant mangled cry travelling towards his organs, to his hands. For days the cry had come to him each night while the others slept, on each occasion, magnified by the constant silence, taut, suffocating. The cry grew in volume, weight, intent. Till he was led by it, until he found himself stumbling outside into the grounds, disrobing by the darkened stream gleaming in the night. Naked, covered in bite marks, he hunched down to catch things from the water; Siamese green lizards who shared an Adam's apple, a piece of jabuticaba fruit which grew another layer of purple skin each time you touched it, one cherub whose eyes had blackened from things it had witnessed upstream, a lung wrapped in cling film. Surrounded by his discontented small audience, Dom Emmanuel removed the cling film, crying as he ate flesh. It tasted like a man he once paid four gold coins in Tenochtitlan to keep him company, to be rough then tender with him afterwards, who had stuck his curious tongue into his armpits as if digging for his body's secrets using a pliable instrument. Dom Emmanuel did not turn around when Filamo moved towards him lifting the blade. The cut to his neck was swift. He fell to the floor, blood gushing. The cry from his lips was familiar. It had been chasing him for days. He pressed his hands desperately against his neck, attempting to catch one last item rising through the blood. Dom Emmanuel died thinking of his lover's sour mouth, praying into it. The wound on his neck a cruel smile, clutching the lines of an old rectory sign bearing Roman number two in the left corner, his talking, gnarled hands slowly eroding. And half his body purple from a winter he already knew. While the monks scattered in shock, the tongue inherited Dom Emmanuel's last words, El Alamein.

When the saints arrived through their time cannon, continuing their ancient tradition as watchmen over the monks, the night was onyx-shaped. A faint howl followed them onto the tower. The Abbey was formidable in the moonlight: imposing, damp, grey, surrounded by high stone walls. The saints were orange skinned from the Festival of Memory. Each had a feature missing but something to replace it within their bodies. Saint Peter was missing an ear, yet had a small, translucent dragon's wing growing against a rib. Saint Augustine had lost a finger on his left hand but had two hearts, one pumping blood, the other mercury, so much so his tongue became silvery at particular angles. Saint Christopher had lost an eye and gained a filmy, yellow fish iris that cried seawater no matter his mood. This time, each had been fired from a cannon. Temporarily deaf, they clutched instructions for short transformations in golden envelopes. They wandered the cold halls lined with carvings and paintings on the walls, while the monks were gathered at supper, oblivious.

The saints deposited the envelopes beneath their beds. Each individual instruction for transformation sealed, yet written in the same long, right-leaning handwriting by the same white feather dipped in blue ink. Each slip of yellow paper wrinkled at the corners, worn from weather, prayer, silence. Then, the saints fashioned three flagpoles from sticks they found in the cellar. They planted them on the grounds. The blue flag for go, red for pause, breathe, green for transform. Afterwards, on their journey back to two golden towers erected between wormholes, the saints became infants in the wind.

Later that night, the remaining Doms filed from the front of the abbey holding their golden envelopes. Dom Ruiz led the way, stopping to take his position at the green flagpole. The other Doms followed. Dom Mendel, slighter than the rest, took a breath on the steps by the Roding's stream. The white hexagon several feet from the flagpoles spun seductively. In the library window, old leather-bound books nursed the wisdom of hands slowly erased by time. The Doms took their positions on all fours. Light trickles of dark rain began to fall. They uttered Pater tollis peccata. Their mouths distorted. The bell rang. They darted forward, towards the centre and each other growling. A sharp, splintered pain shot through their heads. Spots of white appeared in their vision. Bones cracked as they expanded, organs grew, teeth lengthened, fur sprouted, hooves appeared, nostrils widened. Their sense of smell heightened. Dom Ruiz became a boar lunging at Dom Mendel the centaur, chasing him with an urgency that had his teeth chattering. Dom Kamil became an epicyon hunting Dom Augustine the procoptodon between all three flagpoles, through the other side of the white hexagon where the static hissed, then back up again. They snarled at the skyline, leaping, rushing, following the strong scent of old flesh emanating from the soil. They buried their faces in it, leaving large prints around the abbey that had a peculiar beauty from above. Three hours later, they retreated back to their starting positions becoming men again, exhausted bodies heaving. Speckles of blood fell on the golden envelopes, over the lines in foreign hands that had arranged into blueprints.

There were always injuries during a transformation. But the small, morphing nucleuses they had generated would flatten in their brains, rising again when necessary, mimicking the silhouettes of tiny watchmen. As their breathing steadied, they studied the red flag flapping in the wind for stop.

After the transformation, the silence within the abbey was heavier, loaded. Having been banished by the saints for the fallen monk in their midst, each monk was busy dealing with the repercussions of their borrowed hands. And who knew what that could do to a man? Seeds of doubt and mistrust had begun to take root in this fertile ground of the unspoken, watered by the saliva of sealed envelopes. The monks did not venture beyond the abbey, afraid of being sucked into a vacuum of noise they would not recognise. Noises of a future they felt unprepared for, frightened that the influences of an outside world would somehow shorten their time at the abbey. Everything they needed was within the abbey's walls. They grew their own food using the allotment out back. At least twelve chickens were enough to feed from for a while, producing eggs for breakfast and the occasional comic attempt at escape. One chicken laid ten eggs that would not hatch, each filled with a finger of a new monk poking through deep red yolks. Somehow the Jesus figurine had found its way to these eggs. Stained by mud, it sat amongst them as they rolled and the other chickens leapt over the sound. Fed on bits of sullied bread, little Jesus waited patiently for a different kind of resurrection.

The saints made several visits back to the abbey through their time cannon to deliver items: salt, a bow and arrow, a television remote, nails, a hammer, three serrated knives. Several days after the transformation, Dom Augustine woke in the middle of the night barking like a dog, tongue slightly distended, skin clammy. The next morning, he began to set animal traps around the grounds: one on top of the tower, one in the allotment, one behind the middle pew in the prayer room, under his bed, one on the white hexagon slowly fading from damp and cold. After all, who knew what a man's shadow would do while he pretended to look the other way? Dom Augustine felt a panic rising inside him. Each day his tongue loosened further, as if it would fall out at any moment. He did not know whether it was his increasingly intensified barking at nights that was the cause or his particular kink from banishment, from flight. There were always complications. He had arrived in the main chapel, between two tall marble grey pillars, deposited on the alabaster altar, naked and wrapped in a thin silvery film reflecting past angles of light. His limbs had hurt, his head throbbed. His breaths were slow, deep, attempting to acclimatise. He had broken through the film, instinctively grabbing at items from a past that would never appear, knocking over two large, white candlesticks on either side. Famished, he scrambled along the cold altar. He looked down; his gaze met the knowing blue eyes of a cherub who jumped up and down excitedly, showing him its scarred back from repeatedly falling through stained glass windows. Its mouth was purple after eating a combination of plump fruits and unidentifiable things. He'd broken his hands in just like all the other Doms: carving a small Jesus figurine, fixing the hole in the cellar roof, building a pantry. The ache in his hands never fully left, only dulling with time. His fear of items and sounds from the outside threatening to infiltrate the abbey had become so potent, one afternoon he had been washing his hands in holy water by the pantry when the sound of an axe lifting, falling, chopping, breaking, smashing had almost deafened him. Slow at first, coming from afar. Then closer, louder, heavier till he curled up by the metallic bowl of water screaming then barking, breaking the silence.

A week after Dom Augustine set the animal traps, parts of his body were found in each one. Pieces in the traps by the fading white hexagon looked like an offering. The axe the saints delivered had vanished. The tongue in Filamo's pocket dined on splattered blood.

It was a chilly evening on the occasion Dom Kamil decided to perform his act of rebellion against the silence. A light frost covered the grounds, more jabuticaba fruit from the well scattered. Large pillars at the abbey's entrance bore tiny cracks oozing a sticky, thin sap. The intricate, golden chapel ceiling depicting Old Testament scenes began to shed tiny specks of gold from the corners. Only an observant eye would notice the figures had begun to head in the opposite direction. Metallic bowls of holy water carefully placed outside room entrances collected reflections as if they were a currency. Dom Kamil awoke to find himself doused in kerosene and Doms Ruiz and Mendel absent. Throat dry, he trembled before swinging his legs over the bed onto the floor. The smell of kerosene was acrid. He did not call out. Instead, he slipped his dull, weighty brown cloak on, briefly running a hand over the length of wooden flute he'd kept close during the daytimes. For weeks he had found the silence unbearable, craving the joy music brought. He had resorted to wandering around the abbey with the flute he'd made secretly, rubbing his hands along it when his fingers curled and flexed with intent. Beyond the abbey walls, an ambulance siren wailed. Dom Kamil rushed outside, at least fifty yellow notes were strewn on the frosted ground. He scrambled between each one, eagerly opening them but they were mockingly empty. Distraught, he pulled the flute from his pocket and began to play. When Filamo set him alight he did not stop, playing urgently until he fell to his knees, the heat of the flames licking his skin, veins, blinding him. The sound of the flute hitting cold ground reverberated in the abyss, the ambulance siren shattered. A dark curl of smoke shrank into the tongue poking out from Filamo's pocket contemptuously.

The next morning, the two remaining Doms wandered the halls with the taste of kerosene in their mouths.

On the fated Sunday that followed, Dom Ruiz and Dom Mendel began their last set of chores for the week orchestrated by the saints, setting scenes for destruction: ripping the pages of books in the library, defacing the expressions of religious figures in paintings hanging on walls, smashing up the organ in the chapel nobody had been allowed to play, flinging the black and white keys over the bodies of ten monks in the deep, open grave tucked behind the stone steps. They sprinkled salt on those bodies. And when those monks' mouths were sealed shut again by snow from a future winter, they fed the chickens communion. After dying the underside of their tongues purple, they fished out the animal traps, assembling them into a circle at the abbey's entrance because their hands could not help themselves. They danced within the circle until sweat ran down their backs, till their legs ached and the skyline became a blur. The nucleuses embedded in their brains rose, bubbled, spat. They danced for what felt like an eternity until finally they crawled indoors. Heavy eyed and wary of collapsing in their sleeping quarters, they sat across from each other at the long dining table, watching, waiting. They dared not sleep, until the saint in their peripheral vision began to scream, burning bright, burnished orange smog into their heads.

Dawn arrived to discover Dom Ruiz slung over the bell, hands clinging limply to a thick, white rope, face battered beyond recognition. He dangled like a grisly gift a god had despatched. Meanwhile the tongue ran its moist tip along the bruises on Filamo's hands.

Spat out from another chasm, Dom Mendel lay sprawled on a wide patch of the Abbey's green surrounded by concrete paths. Time travel flight had occurred again. He knew it from the trembling in his knees, the ache spreading in his chest, the blockage in his ears slowly thinning, popping. His bruised hands were numb, stiff after being curled in the same position for hours. As though he'd been inserted into a corner of sky trying to balance, fingers instinctively wrapping around the shadows of lost items. Every junction fell off the map each time. A severed organ floating in white smoke till it disappeared. He sat up gingerly, taking small gulps of air. It felt like spring. Bright sunlight shrouded everything. The abbey was a carcass of its former self, its high walls reduced to mere remains. The sound of cars on the roads around it was jarring, alien. Mouth dry, barefoot, he stood slowly, noting the curfew tower in the distance. Exits at either end of the gutted, green gladiator-like pit beckoned. He decided to take the exit in front rather than the one behind him. He crossed some stone steps before landing in the graveyard. St Margaret's church stood to his right behind the tower a short walk away, bearing a flimsy white banner that said Café Open. People passed him throwing curious looks. Their clothing appeared odd and unfamiliar. He ran his hands over a few gravestones. The rough stone was cold to the touch. He grabbed sprigs of grass lining the bases, placed them on his tongue. Chewing, he made his way over the zebra crossing and onto the tail end of the market on East Street, drawn by the buzz of stalls, the cacophony of voices, the smell of meat hissing and spitting over a barbecue. He ran a finger over the tongue in his pocket as he heard the words Bell End, mango, fireworks, truncheon. It curled against his finger as though acknowledging receipt. He walked along the market in shock, throngs of bodies spilling, multiplying and scurrying in every direction. On the high street, a man held a snarling Alsatian back from him. He could smell what it had eaten hours ago, a rotten, pungent scent. He resisted the urge to bare his teeth. Something lodged in his chest. His blood warmed. His heart began to mutate into the shape of the snarling dog's mouth, knocking against chest walls. He stumbled away from them. Trapped light in his retina split into tiny grains. Everything felt intense, gauzy. A bearded man bumped into him. He entered the sliding red door of the shopping centre almost by accident. Things bled into each other; the mannequins' mouths pressed against their glass confines, stitches from their hands coming undone, grazing his retina. Along the way his footsteps were dogged by sightings of familiar faces; Dom

Emmanuel appeared on the raised stage for a concert, holding the knife that had killed him, slicing his neck repeatedly at the microphone. Dom Augustine's head lay in the Asda supermarket freezer, one animal trap snapping over his lost limbs as they reappeared. Dom Kamil sat engulfed in flames in a barber's chair. Dom Ruiz lay slumped over a Thomas the Tank Engine train, clutching one yellow note.

Dom Mendel passed a line of monks on an escalator, touching their shoulders but each one vanished. He was consumed by a loneliness so vast it was unknowable in this lifetime. He followed the exit out and back onto the streets. He kept walking, filled with a slow hypnotic wonder, wiping the dew off a car side mirror, becoming a small figure in its contained distances. Then on all fours, he scavenged in the bins outside the Yaki Noodle bar opposite the station. Afterwards, he walked around back streets staring at houses. He walked to Creekmouth, passing the mural of two men vomiting water, coddling ships while the land flooded. He studied the parked HGVs on industrial roads wondering what they contained, noticing the small factories and recycling stations. A veil of bleakness cloaked it all. The ghosts of Creekmouth swirled. Workers for the Lawes Chemical and Fertiliser Company emerged from rows of cottages attempting to stuff items into his pockets. The Bluebird and the Yellow Peril aircraft of the Handley Page Factory hovered above, between the rough marshland of Barking Creek and the north bank of the Thames leaving white trails in the sky. Children ran from the school, mouths turning to dust as their cries faded. Debris of old lives tumbled through the nearby tidal barrier. The sound of ships sinking filled his ears. An ache in his hands intensified. Laughter from Romanian weddings rang at the entrance of the River Restaurant. He almost entered to search for hands he could borrow. He stood in the midst of it all listening, to marshy land rising, urged by the echoes of the Thames, to the sound of a great flood coming. He did not notice his feet were bleeding. His teeth began to chatter, his tongue distended. The tongue in his pocket started talking.

The last Dom, Dom Mendel, stood on the bank of the river Roding, disrobing to reveal breasts jutting, her nipples hardening in the cold. Pregnant with another bloody season, her new name carved on her stomach from a serrated knife read: Filamo. She had left behind the abbey in the chasm, its entrances spitting Bible sheets, its lines leaning against a distant prayer, the faces of saints morphing into bruises. A different transformation was occurring; malevolent cherubs chased the cockerel, the limping cockerel drunk from holy water chased the Jesus figurine, squawking 'Amen!' Rolling jabuticaba fruit chased the hatched monk's fingers. And the abbey chased new burial ground. Dom Filamo listened to the symphony of cars, human traffic, the beauty of noise. She dipped her left foot into the water. After fishing a hammer and tongue from her robe pockets, she started to bludgeon her head, hitting the ring of hair. As another yolk broke and blood ran down her face, she slipped the tongue into her mouth howling. The tongue of a saint. That first kill. The reason for the punishment of a period of silence. Her skin mottled. She leapt into the river gripping the hammer, chasing the sheep's head that had surely become a different animal by now.

LARA WILLIAMS

TREATS

IT WAS NEARLY fifteen years ago that Elaine had stood peering toward the harlequin bustle of the fourteenth floor, doped by the static September heat, watching the glass panelling refract and scythe. It was one of those sneaky summer days, one that lounges around a chilled August, making a wild and unpredictable cameo, hoodwinking you into knits, swindling you out of sandals. She'd already taken to whispering 'You get to a certain age', to no one in particular; the tiny bones in her hand creaking like violas, shopping bags cutting into the skin of her wrists; whispering it beneath her breath, the words a smooth tonic.

You get to a certain age.

She was thirty-five.

Joan met her at reception, dressed head-to-toe in black, like some sort of devastating widow; her lips a woozy red, her foundation a flawless white facade. They took the lift, staring silently ahead, slim parallel lines, a vertical Hays Code, counting off the floors.

'Hot, isn't it?' Elaine ventured.

'Not especially,' Joan replied, buttoning her cardigan with a pointed elegance.

The office was a mess: a scatter of half-opened boxes, the

cavalier architecture of a child's fort; the ceiling fan flickering off and on; the paint drying in patches. But Elaine saw its potential, the order in the olio, feeling the compact thrill of a nice meal or good art. Her thoughts had slowed to a plod in the heat, circling slowly, like the fish in the bowl her husband had gifted her. She grappled for half-formed ideas; wispy responses dispatched into the air, floating away like dandelions huffed into the wind. To her surprise, Joan offered her the job – Personal Assistant – and she rose to her feet, not quite knowing how to accept the offer, announcing 'Shall I just get us a cup of tea?', a conspicuous affirmation.

She was Officer Manager now, but still retained a few PA duties, picking up dry-cleaning here and there, swirling stevia into coffee. Everyone needed a bit of looking after. Even Joan.

Elaine liked to look out for people. She was a tall woman, and as a tall woman, she suspected she was made for it; made to protect, to watch over. Everything about her seemed to accommodate her height; her airy, echoing vowels, the swooning lumber with which she moved. But then she hit fifty, felt the uteral twangs, the telling hot flushes and fluctuations of mood, and realised her body wasn't made for height, for elevation; it was made, and had always been made, for menopause. She gained a little weight, developing a pleasing paunch she'd rub admiringly. She'd sit at the kitchen table breaking off squares of cooking chocolate. She rang her sister to say she wouldn't be coming home for Christmas, and while she was at it, could she stop being such a goddamn tramp her whole life. She had crème-de-menthe with dinner. She listened to Cher. She booked a trip to the Peak District alone.

Her husband wondered what the hell had gotten into her. He'd curse and rumble, rolling his eyes at her elasticated waistbands, ask her why she'd stopped wearing make-up. But it didn't bother her; things were looking up for old Elaine!

'You want to take an old girl to the cinema?' she asked.

'Not especially.' he replied. 'But I will.'

'Old woman,' he said, after a pause. 'Old *woman.*'

Elaine got in early to leave a plastic pot of maraschino cherries, and a small bottle of vodka, on Joan's desk. Performing secret good deeds was a guilty pleasure for Elaine – a covert joy, a sort of private joke, really, shared only with herself. She would perform secret good deeds, flush with joy, made glad by the baffled delight they'd bring. She'd slip ten pound notes into charity buckets. She'd pay for drinks. She'd order slices of cake, have them presented to young couples, watching them across the café. She occasionally imagined secret good deeds were being performed for her, the world fluent in a silent language of kindness. Upon finding an apple on her car bonnet, a Pink Lady, as yellow and red as the sun, beaming a smiling curve of white light, she thought: Who left this for me? What lovely person left me this? before noticing the rest of the car, a punnet of raspberries smeared across the windscreen, an orange squelched into the numberplate, and a note, tucked and fluttering, beneath the wipers.

Can you keep your fucking car out of the loading bay?

But the slow drag of disappointment had grown numb, hard, like a frozen waterfall, it barely registered. There were things to get excited about in this life. Things to thrill for. Like zumba and sugared almonds. Water aerobics and flavoured liqueur. Cher.

At three she popped out to get Joan some lunch. She selected a smoked salmon bagel and an iced tea. At the till, John the Sandwich Guy, literally the name of his business, slipped a French tart into her bag. Elaine smiled. A big screwball smile. As big and sinking as the Titanic.

'Thanks, John,' she said. 'You're a good egg.'

'*You're* a good egg!' he replied, chuckling floridly. 'An Ananov egg! A Fabergé egg! Eggs Benedict!'

She left giggling, letting the door click softly behind her, and the thought suddenly struck her, as occasionally it did, that she didn't have a single true friend in all the world.

She got home to the smell of pizza, the sound of the seaside, tinkering from the television. She located the pizza box, a paper white square, balanced on top of the kitchen table, promising slicks of grease and steam marbling the lid. She teased it open, knowing already there would be none left, and made instead for the fridge, compiling a plate of leftovers. She ate at the kitchen table, watching the fish circle its bowl, the seventh fish, she thought, Moby-Dick the seventh. She set down her fork to sprinkle fish food onto the water, pink and orange flakes that had the texture and smell of chicken stock. She felt subversive, transgressive, radicalising the food chain like that. The fish wriggled hurriedly to the waterline, its orange mouth nipping sweetly at the surface, its big black eyes frozen in a kind of permanent disbelief, a doubtful and necessary trust.

Once, she had wanted kids. And then she wanted a kid. Then she wanted a cat. But now she was fully committed to this: a solitary goldfish, eternally circling the left-hand corner of their kitchen table. She looked at the goldfish, swimming and flickering, the little hinges of its jaw, chomping up and down. She loved it, she thought, in the smallest, saddest way. She wanted to fish it out, to feel it in her palm, to stroke its slick, twitching body and feel its satin-soft fins.

She finished her food, depositing her plate into the sink, and made her husband a cup of tea. She placed it on the carpet next to his feet, on the flattened pale ring of shag, kissing his head as she went to bed.

'Wait,' he called. 'What do you want for your birthday?'

She paused between the top and the bottom, stasis on the stairs, fingering the covered buttons of her jersey.

'Just your health and happiness,' she replied. She thought he'd forgotten.

'And a million dollars.'

'How about that trip to the cinema?' he said.

'Well wouldn't that would be nice,' she replied, thinking she wouldn't be able to sleep with all this excitement flip-flopping in her heart.

She worked on her birthday. She always worked on her birthday. There were things to be done! – papers to file, phone calls to make. Plus Joan needed looking after: at eleven she would deliver her morning cappuccino; at one she'd remove the cherry tomatoes from her salad; at four she'd make her lemon and ginger tea; past six o'clock she needed to be told to go home. There was a catharsis in it. There was a ceremony. It was a full-time job. It was literally a full-time job! Elaine made time to treat herself too; treats could save a person, she thought. 'Treat yourself every day,' her mother had told her, and she did – taking herself on little walks, an expensive haircut here and there. Once, her husband had treated her, courted her, whisked her off to restaurants, showed her off to his friends. Now her treats were reserved for her birthday, and even then, they didn't always manifest.

At the end of the day, Joan called her in, asking if she'd shut the door behind her. 'Don't think I forgot,' she said, beckoning Elaine over.

She thought Joan looked more pale, more delicate in the milky evening light. She wondered if she was getting enough iron. Joan gestured at a brown parcel, tied with string, propped amongst the scattered jetsam of admin on her desk. 'That's for you,' she said, and Elaine began unwrapping the parcel, pulling back the folds. 'What are you doing?' Joan said. 'That needs couriering. Tonight.' Elaine blushed, a hot pink hue, arching her nose and cheekbones. She resealed the package and tucked it beneath her arm. She could drop it off on the way to the pictures.

She removed her coat from the back of her chair, swinging her bag across her shoulder, noticing her phone flashing, a staccato red reminder. Voicemail. Her husband. Delivering a flimsy excuse for cancelling their plans. She returned the phone to its cradle, sat back in her chair and thought about her life. It was like the time she went to an art gallery, expecting something grandiose, something moving, something, perhaps, profound: swampy colours, powdery paintings of girls in profile. Instead she found hokey sculptures, marble penises extending from the corners. Being given salt when you wanted sugar. An olive not a grape. That was it, she thought. That was her life all over.

She waited in line at the cinema; she'd decided to go alone, though her irritation lingered, like a stubborn base note of leather or sage. She looked at the people queuing around her: couples, mostly, but a few people on their own, also. At the front desk she asked for a ticket for herself and another for the young girl behind her, a fellow solo cinema goer, nervously thumbing the lapel of her coat. She asked they just give her the ticket – no fuss made, no details given. She left the desk, her own ticket printed and folded in the palm of her hand. She thought about the young girl, thought about how surprised she might be, about how nice it was to be treated.

She thought about all the nice things people had done for her, from historic dates with her husband to the brief moment she saw that apple, perched on her car; how her heart had skipped a beat like it might leap out of her chest. She thought she'd treat herself to some popcorn, and a hotdog too, taking up the space around her, stretching out her arms and legs, and enjoying the film. She thought about how it was her birthday, and not a bad one at that, and her heart did a little leap on its own; you could do that, to your heart, you could be so kind to yourself you could make your own heart leap.

After all, she thought, what goes around comes around.

DEIRDRE SHANAHAN

THE WIND CALLING

MY DAD MIGHT still be travelling through England in the caravan, raiding the place of what it's got – jobs, money, sites to stop in – but I haven't heard from him in a long time. There were six of us when we started out, then four after Mum died. My elder brother drifted off. In the end, it was me and Dad.

He had his two china cats, a Spanish fan, pictures of hurling teams, and his dog Treacle, whose eyes are dark as muddy tracks. The past piled up, like the sections in our history books, Stone Age, Vikings and Tudors, which we had from school. Comics, photos and games are stuffed in a corner as if we had never left. The way we lived was the way we were, running around on a midsummer evening, frenzied with the excitement of throwing stones in a pond, the hush of trees we sat under to gossip about Colum Brady, tall, with the squinty eye, blonde and eighteen with a dreamy look, as if he couldn't understand what he had been born into. Ever since I saw him on a site outside of Galway, he wore a long coat which came to the ground, scarves free as streams and waistcoats with flowers. Once he wore a cape. Jem thought he was Jesus but I knew he wasn't, because he had no beard. Jem thought a lot of him because he was always giving him balls, jigsaws, and once a cricket bat which he didn't know what to do with. Colum knew about things we only guessed at: the best form for a horse, their price, the names of the stars and planets. He showed us a swing made from a tyre, how we could nick a bike and a string of pearls he had lifted in a jewellers. He led Jem on, telling him things, setting dares, making up stories.

He talked about going to the south of France, to Saint Marie de la Mer, where gypsies came from, their spiritual home. I used to hope I could visit there, because it was warm and different. He knew the names of flowers, trees, hurly teams. I wondered how, when he had never gone to school, never been forced to, but my sister Rena said he must have got it from books nicked from a shop or a library. Dad said he was shifty and too clever and any fool knew that a lad who wore those shirts and thin ties was after something.

After days away, he would bring me a small piece of jewellery, or a stone with a glint, shells or ribbons and laces I could only dream of, for tying up my hair. Cassie, his sister, and Rena plaited my hair, discussing styles, which colour would be best, whether they should brush up the stray strands or let them fall. They kept hair pins between their lips in front of the mirror my father scavenged from a house that was demolished. They contemplated my face and what would suit it, tied clumps of hair in ribbons and set in slides.

They put me in dresses nicked from wherever they went. Preening themselves in the squat mirror, they were going to challenge the world in the dance halls and almost achieved it but that Cassie had a child at sixteen and went to live with a man who was older. Rena was fifteen and said she would never be caught that way and she wasn't, but she never had the chance with us to watch over, especially Jem. He was a lot of work. She taught him the most of what he would need, numbers and letters. When we stopped in country places we used to go walking the lanes for fruit. He would hang on my arm, almost up to my shoulder, swung my plastic bag with his, juices from the berries leaking after us. Thin and wiry, one of the men said, slight as a wave but I don't know. I've only seen waves once from a distance.

When he wasn't around, it was my job to find him, like the time one summer on one of the better sites. I went in the washroom and Colum was with him, flicking water, making Jem dance. Droplets flying, Colum had flooded the floor. I worried we might be kicked out by the warden but Jem got excited and ran out with his towel sopping wet.

Colum said we should get some air. I followed him out while Jem's voice could be heard in the distance. Colum asked if I'd been up this way before and did I know about the river hidden at the side of the canal where the grass was long and the willows threw down their branches?

When we got to the rough ground by the river, he pulled off his tee-shirt and said he was going in. He was so thin there were shadows on his ribs and his belly curved in.

'That colour suits you,' he said, referring to the red and lavender ribbon and it pleased me.

Afterwards we lay on the grass. Putting his mouth on mine, he drew me close and then it was too late. The day was heavy and stunning. He was the river going through me; words, songs; stories from his grandmother. He locked me into him. His fingers lay on my back, fragile as insects, his lips were going lower and lower. He ran his hand on my arm and down my legs as if he didn't quite believe I was there and water shifted. The air was still and loud with noise. A bird rose. I wanted to weep.

'I'm thinking of leaving,' he said.

He wanted to live in one place, be in the country and off the road. Wouldn't he need a job? I asked.

'There were other ways,' he said.

He would go back over where there was more space and he could be free. You could grow your own food, have hens, live in the fields. What about his family? Wouldn't they miss him? He said he didn't care. They'd have to get used to it, his father was a blackguard and the soonest he could, he was going off.

'Would that be now or later?' I asked.

He said he didn't know. He put his face to my neck and fiddled with the plait at the back of my head, pulling the ribbon off. He ran it over his knuckles so that they came white, then dragged it through his mouth behind his teeth. He tied it around my neck, saying it suited me there. His mouth was wet. I thought he would eat me. I couldn't say any more, even if I didn't want him to go; what he did, or wanted to do, was always separate, grown up. I was scared. He wasn't like one of Brid Canty's boys who were in a remand centre after terrifying a shopkeeper with a knife. They were always out of control though once Brid said at least her sons were men and not the like of other fellas wearing clothes the colour of petticoats.

I couldn't breathe. He eased himself up, brushed his hands on his trousers and looked across to the waste field where we had the parties. He wanted to go there, and would I come? I said I was expected, for there wasn't anyone to cook, so I replaced my clothes, rearranged my hair and carrying my shoes walked back across the ragged grass. I watched him that night from our small window but drew the curtain and got on with washing the cabbage. That talk, notions of leaving unsettled me.

Next time I saw him, it was outside and November. The men had made a bonfire and slung wood onto the rubbish so Rena, Jem, Dad and me stood in the warmth of the flames until the fireworks started. When the drink was gone, there was music and when that was done, singing. Voices seared out, 'The Wearing of the Green' and 'The Croppy Boy'. Words fizzed in my head. Jem gathered the lids of bins and hit them with sticks. Two years younger than me, he had always been bolder. Rockets shrieked into the sky, sequins of pink and blue thrown into the dark. Stars were falling. That was the last I saw of him.

Afterwards, when Dad went to pieces, a family took me in but I never got used to them. I still can't live in a house, something to do with walls, one room leading to another, so you can't get out. One night, I woke to a fierce howling. It was the the flutter of birds in the eaves and the wind, so strong, like a child calling.

They let me go back today, but he drifted, saying he couldn't bear the closeness of cities. He was cramped. He didn't bother to find work. There was no point, everything he wanted, or valued or prayed for had sunk. When he came for me, the strain on his face told more than I wanted, Jem wandering off that evening and not being seen since. It was never the same again. Dad started drinking and said Jem had escaped into the air on wings and he wished he could join him. I had dreams of my father, the rosary passing through his hands, purple beads like blood, the cross falling, repeating the words in a low murmur.

Rena left. She had an eye for the road. We got a text from the coast, then Birmingham, Liverpool and Leeds. She was working her way from us. I had to read and re-read the words to him. The last time she wrote she had got a job, in a salon, she called it. I sat on my nails so as not to bite them, hoping she would come home.

I'm in a job like hers, though I look after flowers not hair. I am gardener or I want to be. I got that from my mother, liking gardens and plants. Dad said the hanging baskets were her idea. They were not strong, only plastic, so the holes kept getting bigger until they rotted. The strain was too much and telling so Dad had to take them down.

I want to see Dad. He could be anywhere, up north, in Scotland, maybe gone back over. When the weather was good he wanted to be there, stalking the fairs, looking for cattle. I see him journeying but lost. I'd like to tell him how I ran into Colum in Balham and how he said he recognised me by the back of my head and my voice. Sitting on a red plush seat under a picture of Queen Victoria, he rose to kiss me, as though it was days, not years, since we met.

He told me Cassie was still on the road but with another man and three kids. I asked what happened to his clothes and he said they were not needed on the buildings. He smiled that nice wide smile but he had changed. His face was harder and tanned. I read lines in his brows and round his mouth. Time had got him. He was in a room in a tall house with small windows but as soon as he got money he was off, he said. That could take a long time, I said.

'As long as it takes, I'll wait,' he said.

I asked what had been bothering me for years. Jem. Colum looked into his drink. The silence lasted years. He fiddled with the beer mat, passing it between his fingers. He said he went to the river that evening. Jem had arrived up saying he had a good pile of cans and he was going night fishing. He asked Colum if he wanted to go along. Colum said he hadn't time and it wasn't his idea of fun, sitting around in the wet dark waiting for a fish to decide to bite. They had a row. Colum had said Jem was a young pup not fit to be out on his own. Jem said he had seen Colum and me by the willow. If Colum didn't give him the price of a bottle of whiskey, he'd tell our dad. Colum told him to head off.

That was the last he saw of him, Jem wearing a long dark coat, carrying a rod and his bag. Later he heard of men seeking him by the fields and the canal, all the way to the river. It was lugged up with leaves, rotting pieces of wood from old boats, heads of elderflower glowing their clouds of white, cartons, dust, shadows and leaves, floating downstream.

DAVID ROSE

ARIEL

CROSS-HATCHING OF BRANCHES against the sky; a Beatles song warping the urban night . . . How little it takes to conjure his shade, dissolve the years.

I hear his whistling in the washroom echo the tune I didn't then know. I lagged behind in everything.

It was 1965, my first job. I was sixteen, spotty and shy. He was . . . I never knew how old Keith was. Thinking back, he couldn't have been so very much older – three years, four, maybe more. But he was a world ahead. He was part of the adult world I was sidling into; he was what I aspired to be. Even his spots were swarthily sophisticated.

I apprenticed myself to him: his way of knotting his tie, of leaving his collar button undone, the way he draped his jacket, matador-like, across his arm – I took careful note. How I envied his accent, his easy adenoidal 'Roight, wack!' We all affected Liverpudlian accents in those days, but ours were ersatz; his, I knew, was the real thing, his living in Slough a temporary aberration – he couldn't have been born there.

It was hard work keeping up. I had just mastered the tie and saved up for the Chelsea boots when he soared ahead again – into leathers, zipped boots and helmet: he had bought a motor-bike. It changed our lives.

A white Ariel, it was, its distinctive front forks the classiest thing I had seen. It would be there when I arrived in the mornings, parked beside the bike shed, still quivering. I would lay my hands lovingly on the petrol-tank, squeeze the brake-lever and dream.At five o'clock, I would watch him donning his jacket, zipping himself in while I held his gauntlets, squire to his leather-clad knighthood. Following him down the stairs, I would listen enviously to the click of steel-shod boots.

Then, while he mounted and spurred the Ariel, I would pedal off frantically to reach the road, knowing he would roar up behind me, throttle down, and with a hand on my shoulder, propel me along until, at the roundabout, with a shouted 'Roight, wack, see yer tomorrer' he would roar off, leaving me prey to inertia.

One day, I let down my back tyre, pretending a puncture, hoping desperately that he would offer a lift on his pillion. He offered to mend the puncture. 'Looks like a dodgy valve,' he said with an expert glance, and slid on his gauntlets. I was glad, though, afterwards. Something would have subtly changed between us. How could Pegasus have a pillion rider? My place was still pedalling forlornly behind. Besides, I would have a bike of my own one day – I was already saving. Not a white one, though, not straight off. I would graduate to that.

Something did change that summer, but in a different way: Keith bought another bike – a Thruxton 500cc – a racing job, and a battered van, transporter-cum-workshop. I felt then that I would never catch up.

Weekends he raced at Brands Hatch. Monday mornings I would be caught up in his cloud of esteem, sitting on his desk as he relayed the race to the Accounts Department. One race in particular stands in my mind. As the flag went down, he couldn't get started; he had to run and push, the engine turning just as the leaders caught him up. He joined them, edging into the pack. At the finish, he was placed third. Nobody realised he was one lap behind. In my eyes, that put him indisputably first, his mocking insouciance worth any number of hollow legitimate wins.

I was settling into work by this time, with gumption enough to enter the typing pool alone, to flirt, even, with the post-girl, secure in Keith's patronage. Suddenly, his hand was removed. With a cheery wave and a 'Roight, wack, be seein' yer' he left the firm.

Looking back, I realise that was just what I needed. My apprenticeship was finished. After the initial inertia, I picked up speed on my own account. I would slip off my cycle-clips and click up the stairs, jacket coolly draped over one arm. I would whistle 'Eleanor Rigby' in the washroom. There were school-leavers to impress, typists to take out. My confidence, though feigned, was effective. I knew I would always be one lap behind, but no-one seemed to notice.

I was still saving hard. Eventually, I did it – my own motor-bike. Not an Ariel, but a Triumph Tiger Cub. Still, it was a start. Nobody rubbed neatsfoot oil into leather with such voluptuous pride as I.

I commandeered Keith's parking space by the bike shed, my oil-drip mingling with his on the asphalt – we were now blood-brothers. At five, I would click down the stairs, wink at the juniors, and with practised nonchalance, kick up the prop-stand and swing astride.

I was now fully fledged. My spots had dried up, my confidence increased to the point where I now carried a spare helmet and offered pillion rides to typists. One of them accepted. She would giggle and wriggle up her mini-skirt, holding me tight round the waist as I roared off, waving to the lad from Stock Control.

That Christmas, I traded in my Tiger Cub for an Ariel.

I was to see Keith just once more. He came back to the office to see us all, above all to show us his pay-slip. He had a job at Ford's in Dagenham. On a good week with bonuses, he earned as much as my monthly salary. He took us out to the car park. He had bought a Jaguar.

My story now becomes a very ordinary story: I married my typist, sold my Ariel, bought a maisonette, then a semi-detached.

But Keith, again, was a world ahead.

It was some years before I learned of it. A clichéd story, but far from ordinary.

A dark night, a souped-up car, an oily road, a placid tree...

And me? I still have ahead of me maybe twenty years of slow, frantic pedalling.

CLAIRE DEAN

IS-AND

SHE WAS THE only one watching - nose against glass - as the ferry navigated the turbines. They swooped noiselessly, churning sea and sky. They looked more delicate and awkward close up, like gargantuan flowers, and they went on for as far as she could see.

Gareth was sitting four rows back flicking through something on his phone. He'd made it clear she was irritating him, making a show of herself for a pointless view. Other passengers watched the news on big screens or dozed. The ordinary breakfast news felt incongruous in this place between places. The island was only sixty miles from the coast she'd lived on all her life, but she'd never seen it. The guidebook talked of the mists of a great magician that kept it hidden.

As they left the turbines behind, the sea and sky settled into mute bands of grey, but she still couldn't see the island. She returned to her seat and rested her head against Gareth's shoulder. He remained intent on his phone. Hers had lost signal and wouldn't get it back until they got home. Gareth had forgotten to tell her before they set off that he used another sim card on the island.

She reached for the guidebook and started to reread the section of walks.

'You don't need that,' Gareth said without looking up from his phone.

'I like reading it,' she said. 'I just like it. I haven't been before. I'm allowed to enjoy it.'

'I'll show you everything.'

She let the book fall closed on her lap and rested her head against him again. 'I'm lucky to have my own walking, talking guidebook.' She took hold of his hand. He continued to thumb his phone.

She dozed and when she opened her eyes again the sky had cleared to a startling blue. People were lined up against the front window. The island was there and she'd missed it appearing. She tried to sidle in between an elderly woman and a couple of middle-aged bikers. The island was small at first but it quickly became too big to be contained by the window. The view shifted with an accelerated zoom. She hadn't taken in everything about one image of the island before it grew closer and there was more to see.

The table filled the back of the room and she caught herself on a corner as she squeezed into the place that had been laid for her. The tablecloth was crocheted and there were napkins in heavy metal rings. There were only two places set. 'Isn't your mum . . .'

'No.' Gareth piled his plate high with potatoes and peas from china dishes. Gareth's plate held three slices of anaemic-looking ham. She had been given one. There was a bottle of lemonade on the table. No wine. She needed a drink. She could hear the radio from the kitchen, where his mum had hidden herself away.

'If it was a problem us eating here . . . I mean we could have eaten out.'

'No, Mum wanted to cook for us.' He unscrewed the lemonade. There was no hiss of air. No bubbles in her glass. It must have been at the back of a cupboard for years.

The Anaglypta walls were cluttered with paintings. Each was a swirl of garish colours formed into a landscape. They glinted from some angles, but looked rutted and gouged from others. There were more of them, clearly by the same amateur hand, in Gareth's room. 'Are they places on the island?' she'd asked as they unpacked their bags. 'Did your mum do them?' He'd just shrugged.

His room was frustratingly bland. She'd expected posters, old CDs, plastic figurines, some traces of him having grown up here. There were just the paintings, more crochet and a crooked twig and wool cross above the bed. She'd read about the crosses, crosh cuirns they were called, in the guidebook. They used to be put up as protection against fairies. His mum obviously had a thing for them because they were all over the house. On the living room mantelpiece there was a line-up of family photos including several of his brother and him as children, and also his wedding photo. His ex looked young and elegant. They looked happy. Next to it was one of a newborn baby in a blue hat. 'He's beautiful,' she said. 'Why didn't you tell me you're an uncle?' He'd clattered the plates on to the table and gestured for her to sit.

The lemonade left an acidic coating on her tongue. Gareth dissected his ham into long, thin strips before eating them one by one. The meat was cold and left a film of grease on their plates. The potatoes were still hard beneath their roasted edges. 'We'll go for a long walk tomorrow,' he said.

❧

Perched in a wing-back chair by the window she leafed through an old tourist magazine. She was desperate to get out and start exploring, but not comfortable enough to interrupt them talking in the kitchen, or to wander round the house to find where his mum had put her boots. She fiddled with her phone, but there was nothing she could do on it. They were talking too quietly for her to be able to separate many words from the murmur of voices and cooking sounds. She heard him say something about an exchange. 'Way it's done,' his mum said, ' . . . if you want . . . returned.'

The knock at the door made her jump. She half-stood, but Gareth came through to answer it.

'This one must be for you,' a man's voice said. 'I've been keeping it for you.'

'Thanks,' Gareth said, reaching out for it.

'It came in unaddressed. Jack wanted to put it in the back with all the other dead letters. People forget a stamp, or get the wrong address, but I said to myself it's a funny business someone forgetting the address all together. I had a feeling about it so I checked it. I think it must be for you.'

Gareth took the parcel without speaking.

'It took you long enough to come back.'

Gareth pushed the door shut a little too hard. The paintings on the wall quivered. He put the parcel down on the dresser without looking at it and went upstairs. The bathroom door slammed.

The bus was full of locals. The only tourists were a middle-aged couple. They kept passing between them the same guidebook that she had brought. They sat right at the front and almost jumped up at every stop. On a wooded stretch of road the man dropped the guidebook, spilling leaflets everywhere.

'That's what they get,' muttered an elderly woman in front of them.

She nudged Gareth and raised her eyebrows in question.

'They didn't say hello,' he said.

'We went over the fairy bridge? I read about that. You should have told me. I wanted to see it, to get a picture of the sign.'

'Sorry.' He went back to his phone.

'What was that parcel this morning?'

'I didn't get chance to open it. Won't be anything important.'

'It was good of them to keep it for you.' She cuddled into him and glanced at his phone screen.

'Who?'

'The post office. All that stuff the postman said, it sounded like they waited for you to come back. You wouldn't get service like that at home.'

He turned to look out of the window. 'Things are different here.'

The route described so neatly in the guide book didn't seem to relate to the landscape at all. Gareth took the lead on barely visible paths that skirted wild grass on one side and sheer drops into glistening bays on the other. Grey rocks erupted from the sea and she tried to attach them to names. 'Is that one Sugar Loaf Rock?' Her voice was snatched away by the wind. She stuffed the guidebook into her rucksack and tried to match his pace. She hadn't anticipated the astonishing blue of the sea, or the violence of movement frozen in the rocks. Grey cliff faces tilted at savage angles and looked as if they might shift again. She wanted to take photo after photo but she wasn't sure Gareth would wait. Besides, she thought, it was better to look with her eyes, not her phone, and try and hold the views in her head.

When they reached the Chasms, he strode out among them.

'The book said we have to keep to the wall here,' she called. 'It's not safe.'

'I could walk the Chasms with my eyes closed.' He shut his eyes and jumped to his left.

The uneven ground was riddled with what looked like rabbit holes, but instead of a fall into the earth there was a vertical drop into the roiling sea. She edged out a little in his direction, but kept one hand on the wall.

'You can't see them properly from there. Come here.'

She hesitated.

'Don't you trust me?' There was worry in his expression, and something else she couldn't quite read. He could be quiet and moody, but she could tell he was carrying a weight of hurt. He hadn't talked much about how his wife had left him, but she could feel the sadness in him. She took his outstretched hand and with her eyes on the ground she wound her way after him on the narrow path between the Chasms.

They stopped to eat the packed lunch his mum had made them at a high point on what Gareth said translated as Raven's Hill, looking down at the Calf of Man.

'There's another island off to the left in the painting in your mum's living room,' she said, 'but it isn't there.'

He shrugged, his mouth full. She needed a dictionary for his shrugs.

As they continued on the thin earth path she tried to keep hold of his hand. There was a deep quiet between the sounds of sea and the wind. She no longer tried to fill it with words, but collected images: bluebells unexpected on the high cliffs, blackened thorns with feathers caught in them, a sleek hare that crossed their path in an instant.

His gaze kept falling not on the path, or out to sea, but inwards towards the fields and a row of small whitewashed houses.

'What is it?' she said.

'I . . . someone I knew lived there.'

'Do they still?'

'No.'

He looked lost. She reached up and smoothed his hair that was rucked up by the wind. 'I love you,' she said. The words felt heavier once they'd left her mouth. She wasn't even sure if she did yet, or if she'd said it to test what was between them, to call it into being.

He turned back to the path and led the way on.

Light seeped through the loose brown weave of the curtains. He wasn't beside her in bed. She pulled a cardigan over her pyjamas and crept downstairs. The package remained unopened on the dresser. She'd almost pointed it out to him before they went to bed, but suspected that would mean he wouldn't open it. Perhaps he'd opened it when she'd been out of the room, replaced the contents and resealed it. She checked the kitchen, and peered out of the windows at the front and back of the house. There was no sign of him. The house was in a row tucked between narrow lanes. No one passed by. A lot of the houses were holiday lets. She hadn't seen anyone else on the street since they'd arrived.

The padded envelope looked like it had been reused many times. The paper was worn thin in places, battered and crumpled, but as the postman had said there was no address on it. How had the postman known it was for Gareth? There was no sound of movement upstairs. His mum must still be asleep. The weight and solidity of the parcel, the straight edges, told her she was holding a book with hard covers. As she turned it over music started playing, a tinny, lilting tune she didn't recognise. She dropped the parcel on the dresser and stood holding her breath. There was no movement upstairs; the sound mustn't have carried. She picked it up again. The flap lifted easily – so he had checked the contents, or his mum had. She eased the book out. It was a baby's board book of nursery rhymes. There was a panel with three shapes to press for different tunes – 'Twinkle Twinkle Little Star', 'Mary Had a Little Lamb', 'Three Blind Mice' – but the tune she'd heard hadn't belonged to one of those. She turned the stiff pages. There were letters that had been blacked out of words here and there. Footsteps on the landing forced her to slip the book carefully back into the envelope. She rushed across the room and picked up the magazine she'd read cover to cover the day before.

His mum just nodded at her as she came down the stairs and then crossed into the kitchen. She could see where he got his communication skills.

He didn't return until mid-afternoon. She flicked through the magazine again and again and again, and drank the weak tea his mum kept placing on the coffee table for her. 'Gareth had to nip out to sort something out. He'll be back soon,' was all she'd say about his whereabouts, and then she sat in silence working on her crochet.

Feeling the day slipping away, she considered going out, but with her phone not working he wouldn't be able to contact her. She kept thinking about the baby book. Why had someone sent it to Gareth? The postman must have been wrong. It was meant for someone else. It had to be, but why were the letters blacked out?

She waited until his mum was making the lunch and then eased the book from the envelope again, taking care not to touch the buttons. She looked for a pattern in the letters that were missing, and tried to make them into words: w . . . e . . . w . . . a . . . n . . . t . . . t . . . o. The kettle had boiled. Plates clinked against a work surface. She put the book back and sat down just in time.

'Did you do the paintings?' she asked as they both ate their salmon spread sandwiches.

'I was taken away after I had Gareth. It wasn't unpleasant where they took me, but I wanted to come home.' His mum clung to the tiny cross at her neck as she spoke.

Unsure how to respond, she nodded and pushed more of the sandwich into her mouth. It must have been some kind of art therapy. Gareth hadn't mentioned his mum had ever been unwell like that, but then there was more she didn't know about him than she did.

'Gareth's father took so long about sorting it out I thought he was going to leave me there for good.'

'They're nice paintings,' she said. 'Very vivid.'

'Have you ever held a changeling? They have a cry that could scour the heart from your chest.'

Wishing she'd never mentioned the paintings, she looked down at the magazine as though concentrating on an article about the island's kipper industry.

His mum collected their plates and left the room, but her voice came through from the kitchen. 'Just because a thing's happened once, folk think you'll be safe from it happening again, but life isn't like that. There are old patterns to follow.' She returned with more tea. 'Kaye's such a lovely woman. She knew what she had to do.' Cold, milky water sloshed from the cup as she set it on the table, her hand shaking. 'I'm sorry, I'm not supposed to speak to you. He's a good boy, though, my Gareth, I won't have you thinking otherwise.'

'What if we booked into a hotel as a treat for our last night?' His mum was in the kitchen, but she wasn't trying to keep her voice down.

'What about Mum? She would be devastated.'

'I'm sorry, it's just . . . This is our first time away together. We've hardly done anything. I've spent most of it in your mum's living room...'

'I told you I'm sorry, the errands took longer than I expected. And you know what, Mum's done everything she can to make you feel welcome.'

'There are photographs of you with your ex all over the place.'

He lowered his voice at the sound of pans clattering in the kitchen. 'You know I was married. I've never hidden that from you.'

'Kaye's your ex. Your mum talks like she's . . . and where is she anyway? Does she live on the island?

'She's away.'

'Were you seeing her today? Is that what you were doing?'

'No.' He headed for the kitchen and his mum, forcing her into silence.

He was asleep with his back to her, or feigning sleep. The light through the curtains woke her at dawn. She waited as it brightened a little in intensity and then slipped out of bed. She dressed in yesterday's clothes without washing for fear she'd wake either him or his mum. Taking an apple from the bowl in the kitchen for breakfast she crept out into the empty lane. Giddy with the sudden sense of freedom she half-ran down the street into the next. He would wake and find her gone, just like she had with him the day before. He'd realise how out of order he'd been. He'd try and make it up to her. He'd explain what on earth was going on with his mum. She'd stay out just long enough to make him worry, but return in time for them to spend the afternoon together before the ferry home.

In the window of a grimy-looking cottage a crosh cuirn leaned against the glass. There were leaves caught in the old wool that had been used to tie it. She passed an antique shop and a pretty little café, but both were closed. The thick dust on the vases in the antique shop window made her wonder when it had last been open. She wandered the long lanes until the early morning damp started to make her bones ache. Another café she passed was closed, but the door to a quaint-looking bookshop stood ajar.

Inside, the shelves were dense with browning books. An elderly man was half-hidden behind piles of books on the counter. He didn't seem to notice her come in. The titles on the spines of many of the books were too faded to read. She picked out a slim book that was the blue of the sea, *Fairy Tales of Mann.*

'Have you a special interest in...' the man looked up and nodded at her, 'because if so I've a number of titles you might like.'

'Do you mean fairy stories? No, thanks, I'm just looking.' She flicked through the volume and stopped halfway. There was a story with blacked-out letters, *he wh-stled a soft tune, and touched her shoulder, so that she would look round -t him, but she knew if she did that he would have powe- over her ever after.*

'Excuse me,' she said. 'I've seen another book with letters blacked out like this. Is it some kind of traditional thing?'

'No, I've only seen it twice before.' He held out his hand to take the book. 'It's a story about a lhiannan shee too, apt choice...' Her expression must have shown her ignorance because he went on as if telling a story to a child. 'If you so much as glance at one of Themselves you're under their spell for good. They'll have you dancing off into their fine halls under the hill.' He looked up at her as if considering whether to carry on or not. 'From time to time some of their things turn up. I think they let them slip through for mischief. They look just like our books, our paintings, our records even, but there's always an extra story, or a curve in the hill that you'd swear isn't actually there, or a tune you've never heard before – something not quite as it should be.' He shut the book and put it beside the till. 'I've gone on too much. Forgive me, they're old tales, and I'm an old man who spends far too much time shut up with only books for company. Are you with us on holiday?'

'My partner's from the island. It's the first time I've visited.'

'And have we treated you well?'

'Yes, thanks.' She pulled her coat around herself, readying to go.

'Have you been to see the Laxey Wheel?'

'No. I've not seen as much as I'd wanted to and we leave this evening.'

'Well we'll see you again, I'm sure.' He picked up the book. 'Would you like this wrapping?'

There was no sign of Gareth back at the house. His mum was in the kitchen baking. The parcel remained in place on the dresser. She pulled the book out and worked her way through the pages: w . . . e . . . w . . . a . . . n . . . t . . . t . . . o . . . c . . . o . . . m . . . e . . . h . . . o . . . m . . . e. She shoved the book back into the envelope and dropped it on the dresser, setting off the tune for 'Three Blind Mice'. It had to be some weird trick his wife was playing. And that's where he kept sneaking off to: he was seeing her. She headed upstairs to pack. She pulled open the top drawer. Her clothes had gone. Her bag wasn't under the bed. Her washbag wasn't on the windowsill. His stuff was all still there. His rucksack was in the wardrobe. Had he packed for her?

She ran down the stairs and into the kitchen. 'Where's Gareth?'

His mum didn't look up from her mixing. 'He's just nipped out to finish sorting something.' She stirred faster and faster. The bowl was full of broken eggshells.

Out in the lane there was no sign of him. She didn't know where to begin looking. At the end of the street, just as she was about to turn into the next, she heard whistling behind her. She'd never heard Gareth whistle. It was the same lilting tune she'd heard from the book the first time she'd opened the parcel. She turned, furious, ready to yell at him, but everything within her stopped. The stranger held her there with his gaze. She took his outstretched hand and let him lead her away.

ELIOT NORTH

THIS SKIN DOESN'T FIT ME ANY MORE

THE ANIMAL'S HEAD emerges from a polished oak shield, red-brown pelt stretched over bony skull. The shield is tightly gripped between my Dad's hands. It is heavy. The veins stand out on his neck as he braces the weight against his thigh.

'What do you think?' he asks.

Ed peers cautiously behind the shield and then walks in a circle around it.

My reflection sits within two glass eyes.

'You can touch him if you want,' Dad says.

My hand reaches out to the animal's nose. It is unexpectedly dry and hard. I trace his nostrils with my fingertip. On his neck the hairs feel coarse and prickly against my palm, but near his ears they are soft and whispery, moving slightly when I exhale. He smells of polish and heather.

'Do you think your mother will like it?'

Ed nods, so much that I think his head might fall off.

'He'll look handsome, I think, on the wall by the half-landing.'

I look at Dad. The half-landing is just a few steps from

my bedroom door. I pull the skin up on the back of my hand and then let go.

Ed reaches up to grab an antler. Dad gently removes his hand, prising his fingers from the ridges of bone. 'Careful now, he's very old.'

I look at the silver plaque at the bottom of the shield and read the words engraved there: *Alfred Kingsley, from Kathleen M. Preedy, Sept. 25th 1912.*

'This woman,' Dad says, 'was a huntress. She must have shot the stag and kept his head as a trophy.'

My eyes open wider.

'I wonder what Alfred made of it?' he says.

I wonder what Mum will think.

'Right, you two, we need to hide him. Your mother must know nothing about this. It's a surprise.'

We smile. Surprises are fun.

'I've asked Nicky if we can put him in her bathtub,' he says, as the three of us troop out of the back door and over the road to Chestnut Square, Dad carrying the stag in front of him. It's freezing outside. Drivers slow down as we walk along the pavement, craning their necks just to see.

Nicky answers the door. She gasps when she sees what is in Dad's arms.

'Blimey,' she says, 'you weren't joking.'

We follow her upstairs, all of us in a line, and put the stag in the spare tub, crowding around to watch as he is lowered in. He looks strange rising up through the white enamel.

'She'll not be expecting that for Christmas,' Nicky says.

'No, probably not,' Dad says.

After we've hidden the stag Dad spends the next few weeks

steeple-jacking and clearing the chimneys. While he works he tells us how the jackdaws build their nests in the spring, dropping twigs down until one lodges and then dropping more until a nest is formed.

'Jackdaws are one of my favourite birds,' he says, 'really bright. Not as threatening as crows or rooks, or as noisy and aggressive as magpies.'

We watch as he pulls down all the compacted twigs to clear the flues. When he is finished he sets off a blaze in all the fireplaces downstairs. Flames leap up and illuminate our faces as we run from room to room, giddy with heat and destruction.

Soon after, snow begins to fall, big, fat, swirling flakes that drag power cables down all over Warwickshire. For weeks we eat by flickering candlelight. Dad ventures out for supplies in the big red Toyota pickup. Our house is the only one in the village with heat. Nicky and her children Ben and Katie write their Christmas cards at our kitchen table, soup warming on the Aga. Copper pans full of water are placed on the hotplate to heat. Ed and I still share baths so we pile in with Ben and Katie in the big tub, Mum and Dad and Nicky forming a warm-water chain from kitchen to bathroom.

By Christmas the snow has mostly melted and the lights are back on. Dad unveils the stag to Mum but we never know what she says. What we do know is that he's staying. Ed and I watch as Dad fixes brackets to the wall. We cover our ears against the sound of the drill, plaster and brick dust falling around our feet. When he finally lifts and hangs the shield, the stag looks like he has always lived there. His antlers branch upwards into ten white-tipped points, ears pricked beneath them and nose blackened with varnish.

Dad looks down at us from the top of the stepladder. 'They

call this the brow,' he says, pointing to the first tier of antlers, 'then the bray and the trey,' he continues, indicating the second and third tiers. It's almost like he shot the stag himself.

I climb the few steps to the upper landing and turn round.

Ed slides down the banister.

I walk backwards one, two, three paces to my bedroom door and keeping going until I feel the iron and brass bed behind me and climb onto it. It stands over a metre high. As I rest my head on my pillow and look out through the doorway the stag's glass eyes are level with mine.

Dad turns around and smiles at me. 'He's not quite a Royal, only ten. Looks pretty smart, don't you think?'

I say nothing and Dad turns and clears away his tools.

Later Ed comes into my room and asks if I will read him a story. He has the Little Bear book in his hand.

'Only if you lie under the bed,' I say, 'and give me 20p.'

'OK,' he says, and fetches me the coin before he crawls beneath the iron bed with his duvet.

When I finish the story and before I turn off the light I look out of my bedroom door. Glass eyes shine in the darkness of the stairwell.

'Night, Ed,' I say, but all I hear is gentle snoring.

I turn off the light and lie in the semi-darkness. Street lights glow through the leaded windowpanes, my curtains always open. I drift off but wake with my legs tangled up in sheets, pyjamas stuck with sweat. It is still dark outside. I look under my bed. Ed is still there, breathing slowly and deeply. I lie back on the pillow and stare at the ceiling.

Months pass and in spring the house finally releases us. Mum places Persian rugs on the washing line and beats them, clouds of dust rising into the air. In the evenings it is my job to put the geese away, but they scare me. They hiss as I try to herd them inside, opening their orange beaks to show me their pointy black tongues and sharp little teeth. One stupid goose decides to build her nest in the middle of the herbaceous border. We all try to round her up, but she won't budge. That night when we go to bed I know something bad will happen. In the morning I go out with Dad. He walks straight to the nest. It lies empty.

'Here,' I shout. On the green grass lie the pink innards, glistening like jewels. A long tube widening into a sac, all left neatly in a pile.

Dad comes over. 'Damn it.'

'Where is the rest of the goose?' I ask.

'The fox will have buried her body. She'll come back for it later.'

I look down and follow a trail of feathers. On the ground lie two white wings opened like fans. A band of muscle joins them where they have been dissected from the goose's back. They look bigger than I remember. I ask Dad if we can mount them on a wooden shield, to go next to the stag. Wings spread, pinned and wired as if about to take flight.

Dad looks at me.

'I don't think your mother would go for that,' he says, holding the wings in one hand, the entrails in the other. I never mention it again.

By the end of summer I've grown used to the jackdaws clattering and calling, using the chimney like a megaphone. The sounds change when the chicks arrive and I go outside to look at the roof. I can see them nesting on the twisted chimney tops, the adult birds bringing food for their young before the fledglings eventually leave their nest.

One night, a week before I start secondary school, I cannot sleep. The stag stares at me and I stare back as I lie there in my bed. His constant, unchanging presence reassures me. When I wake up the next morning it is dark in my room. I look at my clock. It says 7.15 am. I stare into the darkness, and rub my eyes. My ears pick out a buzzing noise. I push my feet into the blankets and sheets so I'm sitting up. It should be light by now.

I get out of the bed and stand next to it. My eyes are drawn to the window. I move a step closer. A black curtain appears to have been drawn across: it moves and ripples and hums. The air feels thick around me.

I take a breath and inch closer. Two huge bluebottles scud past my head, the sound of their flight too loud. My mouth opens but no sound comes out.

I turn, tearing my eyes from the window, and run from the room.

'Mum,' I scream. 'Mum!'

I run all the way to the kitchen.

'Mum, flies, in my room, all over the window, millions,' I say between deep gulps of air.

She shakes her head. 'It can't be that bad.'

I lead her there and point at the window.

'Oh, bloody hell,' and then I know that it's bad.

Mum turns, and mutters something under her breath. I follow her as she goes and fetches a can of fly spray and the hoover. Then I stand behind her and watch as she enters the room, armed like a gladiator going in for the kill.

For weeks my bedroom smells of fly spray and death, even with all the windows open. When Dad tears down the paper that blocks up the fireplace a carcass falls into the grate. A baby jackdaw, fallen through the twigs and down the flue onto the newspaper that had sealed the chimney.

'Flies laid their eggs on the dead bird,' Dad says, 'and then the larvae hatched, and later the bluebottles too. They must have squeezed out around the edges of the paper, drawn towards the light of the window.'

I imagine the maggots crawling over the dead bird.

'I'll seal it up properly this time,' he says. 'No more flies, don't you worry.'

The flies that hatched out from the maggots flew past the end of my bed. I am not comforted by Dad's explanation. He doesn't seem to understand, so I decide to take a bath.

I watch the big tub as it slowly fills, and pour bright blue Radox under the taps. Dipping a toe in first to check the temperature I inch myself in, my skin turning red where the water touches it. I submerge my head and try to forget the flies. My body feels different, like it is not my own any more.

I open my eyes and sit straight up, waves crashing against the sides of the bath.

My brother is standing there, about to ask me something.

'Get out,' I screech. 'Get out,' I slam my hands down. 'Get out, get out!'

Water and soap fly into his face.

Ed turns away, eyes swimming and face screwed up with rage as he runs from the room.

I stand up and get out of the bath, my arms and legs shaking. Bubbles cling to my scalded skin. I grab a huge white towel from the rail and wrap it around me before I go to the door and lock it with the old rusty key.

When I turn around and catch my reflection in the mirror my face appears twisted, my upper lip curled. I open the towel and stare at my reflection. Dark hairs grow where there weren't any before. Buds have sprouted on my chest. I quickly close the towel, two pink spots forming on my cheeks. I check the door is locked before I get back in, willing the flesh to melt from my bones as I add more and more hot water.

I stay there and let the water cool. Minutes, then hours, pass by.

My skin wrinkles; I like how numb it feels.

Mum shouts through the door at me. I ignore her.

JAMES KELMAN

WORDS AND THINGS TO SIP

I HAD TO move on. The main question concerned Anne: where was she? I gave up the highstool at the bar and carried my drinks and bag to a table, accompanied by my brains. That was alright; I needed them to think and I was wanting to think.

The nature of the thought, the content. Forget one's father. Had I been thinking of my father? Not in so many images, simply a sensation, a sensation of daddy – poor old fucker, dead for the last twenty years. We think of the dead, even fathers, they are always with us. Even when we are thinking about all these hundred and one different and varied matters, business matters: will one ever make a sale again in one's entire miserable existence? Shall I ever walk into some fellow's office and chat him into an irreversible decision in regard to a sum of money large enough to guarantee one's job for another fucking month. No wonder one sighs. My old man never had such crap to put up with. He was a factory worker. One contends with all sorts, all sorts.

Life is so damn hectic, especially the inner life. The dead and the undead. And thoughts of Anne and myself, our relationship.

I groaned again. These days I groan out loud. People hear it and look at me.

I didnt need pubs like this in which to become annoyed. Although they did annoy me. I get annoyed at myself, by myself and for myself. Leastways irritated, I become irritated, breathe in breathe out.

Having said that, I was turning over a new leaf. The short-tempered irascible chap had gone forever. Recently I had been prescribed aspirin; anti-coagulants. One's blood. Henceforth I was to be a changed man, a veritable saint of a fellow. Never more would I lose my temper over something as trivial as bad service in a hostelry of questionable merit, a bad boozer in other words, who cares? Not me. Never more. Those parties who ignore a body they perceive as a stranger. Erroneously as it so happens. Little did they know I was a fucking regular so why not treat one as a fucking regular? Who cares, of course, me or not me, it dont matter.

Unpunctuality whether in barstaff or one's nearest and/or dearest.

A bad choice of language. But never more, never more.

What never more? What the hell was my brains on about now? These whatyacallthems did not deserve the name. Brains are brains. Whatever I had, tucked inside my skull, those were unclassifiable, certainly not fit to be described as 'brains'.

Oh god, God even.

Yet Anne was rarely punctual. Why worry about one's nearest and/or dearest.

Odd. I recognised where I was sitting. This was where I typically sat in this typical bar, of all most typical bars. It was side on to the door, avoiding unnecessary draughts.

I had books and reports, the smartphone alive to the touch,

even sensing the touch. And an old newspaper too, a – what the hell was it, a something *Planet* – what a name for a newspaper! Was that not Superman, here at the *Daily Planet* with Clark Kent and that old chap, the irascible editor, what the fuck was his name? Who knows, who cares, Perry Mason or some damn thing, so what, I could have read the sports pages.

Maybe I would. Whether I did depended. I was drained – drained! Yes, washed out, exhausted, weary, deadbeat, shattered; stick adverbs in front or behind, all you like any you like; mentally, psychologically, physically, sexually, emotionally, socially; then quantify: totally, wholly, almost, just-about, a small amount, very much. Had I strength to spare I might read a report, book or newspaper. Alternatively I could sit and sip alcohol, insert the earplugs and listen to something, something! Or view television, or watch the world go by, neither intrigued nor bored by thoughts of a downbeat nature. Mum too – if it was not the old man it was her – why was I thinking so much about my parents? Maybe I was about to drop dead and that was a sort of roll-call of one's existence. Hells bells.

Anne would be here soon anyway. It did not matter if she were late. I had not seen her for six weeks, had not slept with her for my gad three months, three months. One could ruminate upon that. I enjoyed lying with her side on, her eyelids flickering. She also with me. Twas our favoured position. We relaxed. I did anyway, being without responsibility for eight or nine hours, barring texts, emails and even phonecalls for heaven sake, but I could not switch off the phone, though her breasts, her breasts.

I disliked myself intensely. Nevertheless, one continues to exist. A small something in my pocket. A piece of jewellery nonsense for the one I loved. Gold, gold I tell you gold! I screamed it hoarsely, in the character of a crazed Humphrey Bogart, unshaven, unkempt – what was the movie? the mountains and gold.

Anne liked gold. Women do like gold. Golden jewellery. Joo ell ry. I kept the piece in my trouser pocket that none might steal the damn thing. England was not Scotland. Given that forgetfulness was a greater risk than theft. If I took it out my pocket I would forget to return it.

But I did enjoy gazing upon gold. Gold was a pleasure of mine too given that in my position I could not aspire to the unkempt unshaven look, being as how the state of one's dress, the label on one's suit, the subtlety of one's timepiece

Oh my dear lord. Panic panic panic.

Defective memory banks. The mind dispenses with petty data. The clock on the wall. I checked my wristwatch against it, and the phone checking both, pedantic bastard. And not panicking. Never panicking. Never, never never never. I was not a panicky fellow – never used to be – besides which the anti-coagulants, lest the dropping dead factor . . . Jesus Christ I groaned again! I was glaring, why was I glaring? I studied the floor. One's shoes. One's socks. Tomorrow was Monday and I would buy new ones, new socks.

Oh god god god.

Three gods = one God, the way, the truth etcetera etcetera, breathing rapidly several intakes of what passes for air, for oxygen because one's head, one's brains, what passes for the thingwis, the whatyacallthems.

Where however was she? One would have expected punctuality.

And the barstaff:

barstaff are typically interesting. We try not to study them too blatantly lest personal misunderstandings arise. But we do study people. We are people and people study people. Humankind is a reflective species. Two had been serving in this pub for as long as I had been using it which for heaven sake was a long time; seven or eight years. Certainly a long time for barstaff to remain in the job. They assumed they had never seen me before. They were wrong.

But who wants to be a regular? It means one is alcoholic, near as damn it, an alcoholic geek, one who gets sozzled in the same bar year after year.

Neither bar worker allowed me a second glance. I was a nobody. They might have qualified this to 'nobody in particular' which would have been better in the sense that a particular nobody is better than a general nobody. Still it would have been wrong.

Regularity need not operate within a brief span of time; twice every two years is also a pattern, and such an event can be enclosed by mental brackets. I might only have come to this pub six times a year but I only came to the damn town on said half dozen occasions. So is that not regular? Make the question mark an exclamation. Six out of six is not 99% but a fucking hundred if one may so speak. Of course I was a regular. Some people are so constipated their bowels only move once a month. But at least it is not irregular.

That crack once landed me an order. They were feeling sorry for me. Once a month every month is measurable, is regularity. A hundred percent. A man had his dick cut open without an anaesthetic. Having to have one's dick cut open! Oh God. One could only shudder. Without an anaesthetic! That was just like – wow! Why even had it come into my mind! But it is such a fact; its incredible nature has it jump into one's mind apropos of nothing whatsoever. It was in the papers, stuck away on page 7, 8 or 9. It should have been front page news. I must have been reading a quality. Unless it was a lie. Even a sexual disease, a serious one: none requires that sort of operation, a severing of the skin. Getting one's penis sliced open without an aesthetic. Dear lord.

Move on move on.

Sliced was my word, not the newspaper's. It just said cut, cut is cut, sliced is sliced and severing is, of course, severing, he intoned gravely.

One considers punctuality. Why?

The main question: why did Anne even consider a fool like me? It was beautiful she did but why? I was no looker, I was no nothing.

Truly, I was not. Yet she had considered me.

Come the cold light of morning this question continued to arise, to haunt my very being as the author of Gothic yarns would have it.

I had one daughter. We never communicated. She used to tell me the books she was reading but due to my critical commentaries she stopped doing this, and stopped telling me about movies she enjoyed, plays she appreciated, painters that

forget it. The main question, or should I say answer, to our lack of communication

forget it.

The only reliable method of knowledge is literature. I was a reader of books. Truth comes in books: we cannot trust internetual information, nor other human beings, obviously, given the chap sitting at the next table to me was reading a quality newspaper so-called, given that in hostelries of this nature such newspapers, not to beat about the bush.

But what could Anne ever see in me? In the final analysis I was a prick. Upon my tombstone let it be writ: Here Lieth a Prick.

Prick rather than dick; dick is a pleasant term.

In contemporary jargon I would admit to having 'fucked up' my life. One should admit such matters and not conceal them if such issues are thought to be the ones, the main perhaps questions, while Anne herself, she was never a blinding flash, what do they call it, love at first sight, oh this is the girl for me, it was not like that. I was in sore need of female companionship. Males tire me eventually. On guard and have at thou. An acquaintance of mine was fairly camp, well, really a friend rather than acquaintance and not 'fairly camp' but wholly so if not blatantly. Male company exhausted him. He told me that. I was pleased he trusted me enough to so confide. I didnt wonder: how come this guy is telling me such stuff? Rather I confessed to a parallel feeling. He nodded, not at all surprised. I appreciated that somebody else felt the same even although I caught him observing me during a lull in the conversation. I respected our friendship but distrusted it. Certainly there were times male company repelled me. Males are uncharitable. Younger males too, perhaps especially. One would expect tolerance. Walking into some factory or warehouse and them all looking and sniggering, what is he selling, fucking fool.

On occasion I need to sit, only to sit, to sit still, to sit at rest, to just be be be be, just be, and unaware of my breath. Without a woman this was impossible. Another friend was an ex-alcoholic and divorced. He told me the major boon concerning alcoholic friends is how they relax together; they share basic acquaintance, occasionally drink tea together, occasionally not. But they lapse into silence. They do. I found that remarkable. I should have expected a headlong charge into confession, each outshouting the other, listen to me listen to me, the poem of course, who was that now? Coleridge.

Silence. The leaves doth grow, doth shed, falling.

I first met Anne on the other side of town. She was in company. I was introduced to her and we got on. We met the following evening. The sexual attraction was mutual. My heart skipped a beat. What is beat? The assignations began and we lay together. She chose the rendevous. This bar.

Life has the habit of booting one in the testes. Anything might happen. I checked my watch and, instinctively, my belongings. A man had risen from his seat, cigarette already in his mouth, making for the smoke exit. He was a shifty-looking bugger. An older man but older men can be shifty given they are less suspicious, immediately that is. Once one ponders a little one has second thoughts, these bastards are just cautious, seeking the slightest opportunity.

The truth is that I did not care. If someone wished to steal my goods and chattels they were most welcome because I did not give a fucking shit one way or the other and that is to be blunt about it.

I had become an afternoon drinker, an imbiber of false hopes, false dreams. Even one's fantasies are false. What is a false fantasy? I once had a boozy conversation with my daughter. Unfortunately I advised her of my secret desire which, at that time, was death. Nothing false about that.

Oh fuck.

I reached for my briefcase to check the report. I had 'a report'. A REPORT!

Jesus god.

I also had an anthology of short stories by writers from Central America. I left it concealed. Instead I would read the walls and read the tables, read the chairs and read the floor. Truths are where you find them.

I opened the report once again, he sighed wearily.

The sort of fucking garbage one is fed at head office. Not that I cared, I did not fucking give a fucking rat's fucking arse, bastards. Even if they did fire me. I did not fucking care. Not one solitary particle for all their lies and dissembling: should one be cast onto the heap of forgotten souls? Never!

They no longer pretended respect. But I had none for them so there we are. Whatever I had was gone. Such incompetence. They were unable to back a chap! They wanted to sack me but could not. Ever heard anything like that! At my age, all one seeks is competence, efficiency. People who do their work in a consistent manner. They do not fall down. They do not leave one high and dry. They do not forget the most important component of any business. Salute in passing oh colleague. Do not fear. One's hopes and dreams will not fall on stony ground.

It does not matter how gifted the scientists are, how advanced the products, if those cannot be sold they will sit there in the warehouse. These are not planks of wood and tons of gravel. Wood and gravel will be of use in a thousand years' time. For new technologies all it takes is six months, if these cannot be sold in six months let them be consigned to the heap of forgotten ideas.

On a daily basis fevered spasms struck my brain. A customer said to me: William, your brains are palpitating, look! See the sides of your head: your temples are banging together. Look, look at your whatyacallthems!

How does one spell 'forever'?

The new technologies are of a certain order. Technologies do not change things in the world they change the world.

I had a proposal for Anne; not wedlock, of slightly greater importance than that. But she, however, was a woman.

What do I mean by that?

Nought may be taken for granted.

I had one ex-wife and one who – well, the reality, I had been a widower when I married her. My ex-wife was my second wife. My first wife died a heck of a long time ago. So so long ago. Mother of my daughter. Yes I thought of her. Parents, mothers, fathers.

It would be wrong to say that I did not think of her. Yes, I did, after so many years. I no longer felt like her lover because I had been her lover. I carried a photograph of her and had scanned a couple too. My daughter kept most of the photographs. She was quite remarkable really. She had a smile – what would one call it? – beautiful, the most beautiful smile. Girls are so damn open, they are so damn generous! In fact

move on.

Women regard wedlock in a favourable light.

Vodka and water. A typical drink. Not my favourite. A colleague described it as a 'working drink'.

Things that are truths are no longer truths. This type of mental whatdyacallit peregrination. By the time one remembers the context one has forgotten the word. It was age. Ten years ago I would have followed the thought, wrestled from it the sense. My line of work destroys the intellect. I was a university graduate. Now look at me. I glanced round quickly, having spoken aloud. I did. I thought I did anyway, maybe I did not, maybe it was oh well, and if I had, what odds, what odds.

The reader of the quality newspaper appeared to be concentrating unduly. He must have heard me speak.

The reference was freedom. I saw it as a possibility, as substance. When I was a student, many years ago, I lived my life taking freedom for granted, intellectual freedom. Enmeshed in that assumption is the concept 'progress'. Students assume progress as a natural state. A false assumption. Nor, if it does exist, need it be chronological or should I say linear, geometrical rather than algebraic, in keeping with the digital thingwi, revolution.

Vodka and water.

Once a widower always a widower. If one's wife was one's first, one's first love. Not just a relationship, a marriage, complete with child, finished. One wee girl. It was nice having a wee girl.

It was a pleasant drink aside from anything. In the past I used cola which had become too sweet so then lemon, bitter lemon, stressing the bitter. A vodka and lemon please, bitter. Vodka and orange, bitter orange. Gin and bitter orange. Gin and lemon of course. But not gin and water. Why! And of course Spanish brandy and water, I had a fondness for Spanish brandy, if only to annoy the purists.

Drinks that do not stain the breath; which does not refer to the Spanish although it too renders one too eh well now how to say it, pissed.

Life is strange. Context is all. Without context where would we be? Where would the world be? This question is the most real. One might consider much. But, howsomever. Then when the context is human, a personned-entity, another person, i.e. not oneself. When another intellectual being, repository of humanned data, has become the context. Love is indicated.

How does one define love? Anne is not at all in the image of my first wife and yet and yet, needless to state, I, well, perhaps, ah, perhaps, indeed, may I love her, do I love her? do I do I – a song by Blossom Dearie, oh Anne do I love you, do I do I.

essence of woman

Language turns a man inside out. The world through Anne-tinted spectacles; today William is wearing his Anne-tints.

Having said all of that, ignoring reports and briefcases, if not for university I would not have read and appreciated Monsieur Sartre. I did appreciate Sartre. People condemn universities. Not me.

I was so looking forward to seeing her. I had failed to appreciate how much. If she was not going to turn up, and let us face it

Why was she not here? She was not here. She was not coming. Ha ha.

I was not a man for the one-liner. I enjoyed proper jokes. More jape than joke, and japer than joker. I performed japes. Allez oop. Just sign there madam.

Yet when it came to it, thinking about how much time I gave to her, to thoughts of her. Not all that much. I thought about everything else. But she was never faraway, lurked within, inside of the brain old gel, she was at the root, her presence determining negative space. Mine was the most healthy negative space one could discover: so much so it was the opposite of negativity where negativity is an unpositive element. Anne was the direct opposite, and inside my head she was like that. My head had been full of vile bitterness, a composition of bitterness and anger. And rage, irritation and frustration and bloody hurt sensitivity, hurt sensitivity, too much even to think about; such that it drove a man to distraction. Soon she would enter the bar. She would place her hand upon my brow. In a former life she was a healer. Upon the brows of the ill and dying, and they did heal. She has retained this ability through various transmigratory peregrinations. Peregrinations, a damn fine word. I would to construct a monument to my love, this woman of the balm. Vodka and water. I gestured with the glass as in a quiet salute to the dearly departed, the yet-to-arrive.

A bar worker was gazing across. I nodded to him but my nod was not acknowledged.

I was an interloper.

People's lives are sacred.

Through the side window the street lights blinked. It was early December yet still warm. I liked the north of England and Lancashire in particular. Jokes abounded but I found it okay. It was not dull and it was not dreary. Ever stepped down from Wigan Central and not enjoyed a large brandy in the bar of the Station Hotel? Or am I thinking of Rochdale? The old Station Bar had gone of course, like community fellowship, the days of which too had gone, yea. One crosses the road to the licensed grocer as once we termed the mini-market, a half bottle and a couple of cans for the rest of the trip home, perchance one avoids the more obvious error, madly dashing back up the stairs into the station and stumbling onto the slow train to Fleetwood, or Blackpool or where was I when the conductor came calling? Never mind sir.

It was two and a half hours since the text. Anne was most overdue, let us say – albeit her life, her life was complicated.

Other than Anne and my first wife I have had five women as serious presences in my own life, excluding my paternal grandmother with whom I had an early bond. My ex second wife, my present partner, my elderly mother, my daughter and Joan Richmond with whom I had a lengthy affair some years ago. It struck me that these six women, in fact seven – eight including my grandmother – shared characteristics yet nevertheless were so different.

In fact it was eight women. Dear god!

This was predictable.

Eight women.

My daughter did not count being of myself. I was attracted to aspects of myself. Yet at the same time we two were so different! How could we be so different and at the same time be aspects of the one?

Shared characteristics and traits. Such a cliche to say that I loved most all but I did, nevertheless, I did. I do not hesitate to use the word, 'love', for what is love? The indefinable, he said with a cheery grin. But Joan Richmond? I could not have loved Joan. Joan was just

I set down the new vodka and water, what was left of it, very little.

My ex second wife was generous.

My God almighty sometimes it took her ages, bloody ages, we are talking ages. If somebody said to me are you coming and I said yes I would be there in two minutes, but that did not work with one's spouse. Nor did it work with Anne. If she said two minutes it was two damn days by the time she took care of everything so I had to advance her notice beyond reasonable limits. But of course. What was wrong with that? People cannot be expected to drop everything. Especially women; which is no sexist joke. I do not like sexist jokes. Women require greater segments of space and time.

Hells bells.

The shifty-looking smoker had returned to his seat and the door opening again. Whoopee. I was onto my feet and to her, grinning like a madman, taking her by the elbow. Anne Anne Anne. Sorry I'm late, she said.

Oh God, dont worry dont worry. I was laughing now and trying to put the reins on it. I showed her to where I was sitting, assuming she would sit on the chair next to me but she pulled back another, to sit facing me. I waited for her to talk. It was important to do so. She looked so great. She did! She glanced about the room. Same old place, I said.

She grinned.

Oh jees. You are looking wonderful my dear, my god you are, you are, you truly are.

Anne whispered but too low and I couldnt hear. I asked her to please whisper it louder, more loudly.

I couldnt get away, she said quietly, self-consciously. She gazed to the bar and added, You look tired.

I am. I'm going nuts into the bargain: g & t?

Thanks.

Imagine forgetting the damn drink!

I ordered another vodka and water for myself, a packet of crisps and a packet of nuts. I was looking forward to the night, looking forward to a meal. Where would we go? I hoped she would opt for Indian food. She preferred Chinese or Italian. I preferred Mexican or Indian. Grub needed bite. One for the notebook that. I smiled and shook my head. Grub needs bite, I said to the bar worker who didnt reply but smiled vaguely which is always fine by me; if I get somebody to smile then half the battle be o'er, I shall get them to buy, for 'tis my job, the modus operandi.

Anne was signalling to me; munch munch. She was wanting a packet of crisps!

Allez oop. I abracadabrad at the bar where lay the bag of crisps side by side with the bag of nuts. The bar worker smiled honestly while handing me my change. Thank you most kindly, I said.

Anne ate her crisps in a mechanical way. But it was interesting. I was chomping a nut. Nuts for me and crisps for her. Aha! Hey! I said, a wee test.

She chuckled, and it stopped me in my tracks. I had been about to say something but her chuckle, her chuckle. You're laughing at me, I said.

Wee test...! She shook her head, smiling.

My Scotteesh voice senorita eet knock you for seex? Seriously, I said and I snatched the packet of crisps out her hand. Without looking at the packet, what flavour's the crisps?

What do you mean?

Nothing, I'm just asking.

Could you repeat it?

What flavour's the crisps?

Aah . . . Anne frowned for a moment, then studied me. I know it's a trick.

It's not, I said.

Mm. She frowned again. Is flavours a noun or a verb?

Pardon...

Is flavours a noun or a verb? she asked.

I looked at her. She was smiling at me. Anne smiled at me. Her hand was to her mouth, and she reached for my hand and held it, she studied it, turning it palm up, examining it for personality indicators or signs of the future. When do you go away? she said.

Tomorrow evening.

Are you working tomorrow?

I've got to be.

She nodded, she now was holding my hand with both of hers; both of her hands, she kind of cradled mine. My hand. What was I? Just a damn man.

That's why you're here, she said.

I couldnt reply. I was the best part of I think what is thunderstruck because this is what I was and felt like crying and felt as if I could cry right there. The whole of life was too good to be true and I was the luckiest man in the whole world and that is the God's truth so help me my Lord God, the one bright star in the dismal night sky. She was the only only thing. She pushed aside the crisps and studied her drink. She raised her head to look at me but only for a moment.

What's wrong? I said.

She smiled but kept her head lowered. You are always so sharp, she said.

I saw the worry in her. My hand went to hers, rested on it. It was above her nose where the worry was, in line with her eyebrows. I wanted to stroke there, easing it, the burden there. I glanced at the empty seat beside me. Come round here, I said, please. Come round here: sit beside me. She shook her head and continued studying my hand, which I made to withdraw, it was strange to me at this moment. I shifted on the seat, edgily, although there was nothing wrong. If anyone had asked me, nothing.

NIVEN GOVINDEN

WAVES

OF COURSE HE should sleep. Now that he was in hospital, there was no question. The hypochondria from before faded once the ambulance showed up. What was clear is that he should rest whilst the doctors investigated.

— Close your eyes, Jacob. Get your head down.

— Rest, and let us do what we have to.

Sleep is all that he trusts in a body that is failing. For each meal he's unable to hold down, the sheets he cannot keep dry, sleep is the old reliable. He allows the meds to knock him out, regressing to the state of a newborn, illness forcing him to relinquish control and simply fall back onto the elemental tropes of food, rest, and nappy changes. Does he sleep like a baby? How would he know? There is no one around to tell him, his mother long dead, those who purport to love him now nowhere to be seen. He asks whether it is possible for a nurse to watch as he sleeps, to make notes that go beyond monitoring his vital signs, but they mistake this as fear of being left alone, keeping the door of his room ajar as if this will reassure him.

All he knows is that he dreams, a surfer riding opiate waves as soon as they first appear, thrilled by the force of it. His consciousness drifting in and out of a strong tide. Who says he can no longer have fun in bed? He's surfing Waikiki from the seventh floor, holding his own for as long as he can, until he drops and lets the drugged sea take him. He rides to exhaustion, paddling until his arms have no strength to even push the hair from his face, his voice hoarse from screams of terror and elation. On his actual visit to Hawaii, he spent no more than two hours in the water, the time not commensurate with the expenditure on custom surf paraphernalia, knowing even before he'd left the Jeep that he despised the instructor's youthful confidence, how the boy's ease with the sea was impossible for him to master in a series of ten lessons. He could have built a hut on the beach, sleeping out there for weeks and still not control the sickness lodged in the pit of his stomach, a reminder that nature could not be controlled through force of will, that the discipline needed to surf, the sheer bloody-mindedness, was weaker than his lazy desire. So why now does he return here in these empty afternoons, breeze pushing hard against his soft belly as he paddles into the surf, the tenacity to ride and fall, to ride harder and stronger until there is something approaching harmony between his salt-blistered feet, the board, and the waves? Nothing about that holiday made him happy bar how his legs looked in a pair of long floral shorts, yet all he sees as the frequency of the IV drip increases is the sun breaking over the Pacific, his skin slowly warming as he moves from shadow, its tone chasing honey as it leaves its natural white and blue. He recognises that in health these dreams would not come, so that on waking there is a perverse satisfaction, thankfulness for a tiny part of what this illness brings.

— Did you sleep well, love? the nurses ask.

— Are you feeling rested, sweetheart?

Ignoring that he is unable to speak clearly from the sedatives making his throat dry, the bark and scratch of his voice painful to his ears. Instead, a persistent cheerfulness as he is bathed and changed, making him almost wish to be shouted at for being so helpless. He longs for an exclamation of surprise or irritation from those who tend him, if only to break through the wall of impenetrable stoicism. Something to suggest that it remains in his power to change what is happening to him, but there is only this steadying, impersonal efficiency. It is all well and good to be clean, and have your weak muscles massaged to encourage circulation, but how to control your insides, to lower your blood pressure simply by willing it, to clear the impurities in your blood through thought, to eliminate those organisms that multiply and attack your cells? Why do they never explain the contrary nature of hospitals, he wonders? How it is entirely possible to become sicker after admission than before. And in what way does a lifestyle of healthy diet and exercise help him now? One carrot is no defence for what is happening under his skin: the unspeakable wrapped around cartilage and within tissue, seeping into organs, and lodged deep in the marrow.

He would escape if he could, from the room and the smell he cannot help but manufacture. Back on the island, O'ahu, he runs laps around his hotel complex, penance for a lack of aptitude in the water. Running he can do, even with his frame, the ease at which his bulk covers ground, over man-made hills, through copses of manicured palms, their growth meticulously planned to please tourists, past thick bougainvillea, heady with fragrance, the scent so perfect as to appear synthetic. Only his sweat to muddy the air. Something accomplished in the perspiration that soaks his T-shirt, the hammering in his chest as he pushes for one more lap, then another, running to the point of dizziness, the Honolulu skyline visible through the trees, until the palms and the golf course it borders onto disappear into a white void.

There were many simple things he once relied on to take him out of himself: running in the park or propping up a bar; looking a fool by challenging younger men to pool games that were out of his league. Similarly, the test of another vehicle drawing up beside him at the traffic lights, revving his engine and daring a race against a white van or souped-up Fiat crammed with teenagers. Far greater than his pride is his impatience to demonstrate strength or knowledge with those a generation or more behind him, and how this grows with age. The swagger of young manhood a tipping point for his antagonism, which shrinks as his waistline swells. He has a shorter fuse, disintegrating as fast as his brain cells. For all its unattractiveness, the inevitable humiliation by juvenile hands, he is thirsty for these encounters, anything where he can deliver a lesson.

— Rest, say the doctors. It's important that you're comfortable, but we can't progress if you don't look after yourself. Stop looking for arguments with the nurses.

The suggestion being that rest cures all, that somehow all the drugs they pump into him are merely indulgences - a warm-up for the real work that must take place, a remedy beyond the doctor's realm, something undefined and akin to magic. But he knows that his body does not repair during sleep, white blood cells attacking red, bacterial infections running laps past sluggish antibiotics, each race faster than the night before, more destructive, all conquering. You do not surrender to illness, he thinks. You are not given the opportunity, too busy mulling over your chances to realise that you've been gripped by the throat. Illness is a hunting dog that does not shake its prey. Long after he leaves the hospital, he imagines he'll remain in a state of shock, his body withstanding multiple jump-starts and meddlings. The months it will take to fully recover, to walk steadily and learn to keep down food. And everything punctuated by sleep. The promise of sleep. The disappointment then, waking to find himself still in bed, and to a body further destroyed.

A morphine sea pulling him back to the beach, a barbecue set up by the hotel where he drinks one bottle of weak local beer after another until the fizz in his guts sets off a greater fire, his jeering at the hula loud enough to still be heard over the chants and drums, his dancing more unsavoury as the moon over the Pacific grows in brilliance, swelling overhead, as if to project his anger. He looks at his hands gripping the bottle, the skin dry and sagging from his knuckles, wrinkles within creases and spotted with tiredness and dirt. He feels useless and old. Twenty years ago, it was entirely possible that he could have ruled this stretch of beach just by relying on his strength of body and mind. What he has now – aches and pains, clumsy when he'd previously been dexterous, a feral grubbiness replacing sexual allure – brings out the worst in him, his behaviour abhorrent, his language increasingly foul, relishing the sound of his voice as it cuts across the other guests, welcoming an audience despite the clear berth they give him. One of the more fulsome dancers holds his gaze, though she too will reject him later, leaving only the surf instructor to take him by the shoulders and gently nudge him away from the main party.

— Let's take a walk, mate. Get some night air in those lungs.

— You're Australian?

— Only in your dream, mate. When you met me I was Polynesian born and bred.

He's grateful for the rescue, knowing the ugliness he is creating, yet still resenting the boy's good sense and confidence to take control of the situation. How he'll be congratulated as a hero the next morning, an extra bonus at the end of the month, and his pick of the hula girls. His own possibility as a saviour to anyone has long since expired, the injustice sticking in his craw.

— I didn't have to fly halfway round the world to get plastered. I can be an idiot anywhere.

— That I can believe. Let's keep walking. You'll feel better for it.

— Look at you - Hercules in surf shorts. Doesn't last.

— I think it'll do for now.

— You think you're it, son. We'll see.

What strengthens as power fades, resolve or decay? Waking one morning he has difficulty opening his left hand, fingers bunched tightly into a fist as if independently deciding upon their permanent repose. It takes two nurses to uncurl him, one digit at a time, only for it to settle back to its previous form once they leave. As a consequence, he's no longer able to feed himself, spoon-fed by whoever is there. This is not giving up, he thinks. More a pooling of resources. The energy it takes to be disgusted I must use elsewhere. The effort it takes him to stay awake and face his enemy, to stare down his hand and the sallowness of his skin, to grip what is left of his wasted flesh, willing back the days when a combination of authority and pure heft could right things.

He feels his body tense up as he drifts into sleep now, his shoulders hunching when they should melt into the blankets swaddling him, his fists clenched, burning a hole in his palm. He understands the false premise of falling unconscious, that it is neither painless nor restful, and how his body physically resists it by refusing to soften.

— It's not uncommon, one nurse comments to another, unaware that closed eyes do not necessarily mean closed ears. I've seen them get like this before. Natural instincts taking over. Impulses we don't realise we even have.

— You mean, faith?

— More... persistence.

Asleep, yet awake, he's aware that personal power still exists, obscured somewhere deep and impassable, an insect smothered in amber and buried under rock. Falling again, until he's upturned. Back to imagining the beach, his face now at sea level, damp and claggy from resting on sand, exhausted from effort, dazed from a closing punch to the side of the head, locking the sound of waves between his ears. Still, he reaches.

— Look at him knocking his fists together. The concentration on his face. Should we wake him?

— Leave him, nurse. Can't you see this is what he needs? He's fighting it. He's fighting.

DAISY JOHNSON

LANGUAGE

HARROW WILLIAMS WAS the sort of boy who got away with things. Harrow Williams was not fat, only big; built through with power. She was not small-boned herself, you could have that fact for nothing, but what she liked most about Harrow was that he was taller than all the other boys and spanned across the shoulders like a bear. He'd been big when he was a child, violent with it, but had only seemed now to grow into his size. She'd loved him since they were four and he'd leant over, planted a red-paint handprint onto her chest, almost knocking her down. As if he owned her already.

And what sort of a device was she? At sixteen Nora Marlow Carr was good at all those things nobody much wanted to be good at. She could do maths in her head the way other people came up with sentences; remembered pretty much everything she saw written down or heard told to her; knew the ins and outs of string theory and could, if she had the urge, take apart a hefty radio and jam it back together. She didn't sleep much and she knew it made her look like someone had beaten her about the face, but there it was. She was larger than was fashionable; sometimes caught herself looking with something akin to lust at all those bones that protruded out of girls at school; the solipsism of legs and arms, the buds of them. Mostly, though, she thought they looked as if they hadn't grown properly. She understood – because she was logical and somewhat cold with it – that they saw her with the same confusion; imagined her bready with everything she carried, watched with distaste the motion of her childbearing hips, her milk-carrying breasts and wave-making thighs. She was a natural woman, they sang to one another under their breath when they saw her, and meant nothing good by it.

Harrow had worked through those bony women and them through him and she'd watched with dry fascination. In reception, it was little Marty Brewer who was the first girl to have her ears pierced and who held his hand for a day before holding someone else's. Nora listened to the gossip, knew Harrow liked to take a girl on the bus to the cinema in the city and then to Subway. If he liked you enough he'd kiss you on the way back. Later she knew, because she understood about biology, there was more than hand-holding going on.

The year she turned sixteen she decided enough was enough. She was not the sort of girl who waited for something to come her way and, if she wanted a thing bad enough, she thought she could probably find a way to get it. She waited until after sports when all the other boys had gone home and Harrow was out with Ms Hasin practising for the 2,000 metres. He was heavy for a track runner but there was enough power in those limbs – legs more like a horse than a boy. Everybody said he was building himself up for the next Olympics.

She went out into the car park and leant against his car and when he came walking up she looked at him. There was no one else there.

He screwed up his face so lines appeared between his nose and around his eyes.

Nora, right? he said, as if they hadn't been in the same school since they were four, as if he'd never planted that red handprint. Well, that didn't matter now.

She thought the most beautiful thing she'd ever heard was entanglement theory. She told Harrow that was what they were: two particles forever linked and fated to change one another. He looked at her askance and she tried hard to think how to put it into a language he would understand.

When she looked back at him he'd taken his cock out. It was not miraculous the way she'd imagined, not beautiful or serene or possessed of any great power. All the same she liked the strange nod of it moving seemingly unconnected to the rest, recognised it was circumcised and liked that; liked the small, dark spots at its base.

You need me to tell you what to do? Harrow said.

She shook her head. She'd read the literature.

Harrow meant it to be a one-time event and that was a fine thing for him to think, but she knew he didn't really understand entanglement theory at all, only liked hearing things he couldn't comprehend, and that it would be a while longer before they'd shake one another.

She knew the way it worked. She was supposed to be coy and shy and give him her home number and wait to see if he'd call her.

That was one way of going about it.

She rang him the next night until he picked up. Didn't let him speak but told him everything she was going to do to him. When she was done she stopped and let him think on it.

All right, he said.

His mother worked the night shift and her parents hadn't ever worried she was the sneaking-out type, so they met at his. She knew why it was so good, why it was better than everything she'd overheard from the girls at school who spoke about it with a sort of aged disappointment. Because he didn't think he had to treat her the way he would one of the skinny women he'd marry, and she had nothing to lose. Afterwards he gave her the lines he'd picked up from American films and she let him get them out: he wasn't looking for a relationship, he just wanted to have some fun; she was a great girl, she really was.

I'm coming over, she would tell him at school or she'd text him when she was already out the window, sliding down the roof slope, dropping to the grass. Sometimes he said: well, I told you I'm not looking for anything of the frequent-flyer persuasion, or he'd shake his head and say he wished he could, he really did, but his evening had pretty big plans wound up in it. That line only held fast the time it took for her to get her bra off.

When he said it, she knew it surprised him more than her. She let it rest between them for a moment with his face sort of stiffening as if he'd been electrocuted. Then she said: well, yes. Me too. And that was that. Harrow Williams was the sort of boy who only held one state of mind at a time and once he decided they were on, there was nothing he or anybody else could do about it. She told him she didn't believe in marriage, that nothing she was ever going to do was for the government or god or anything else beginning with g and that marriage was just a force of control. He looked at her the way he did when she said things he didn't understand; but after they'd had sex, he told her if she wanted to live at his house they'd need to get it done.

She'd never really given up something for anyone. You could do anything else, she told herself; you could break everything in half and scoop out the middle and put it back in. You could write a book or a play or cure infertility. She was eighteen and school was done and she could go to Cambridge or Oxford or London and study maths or English. She could travel. Except she had time for all that. And she had time for him.

If you don't want to marry me you don't have to, he said, a little sulky with it.

I do want to. OK?

Yeah. OK.

Her parents didn't like to argue but, after she told them, she caught them studying her face in a sort of confusion. As if they would discover, looking hard enough, the trick of the matter, the deal she'd been forced into. As if she would slide a note across to them if they waited long enough and it would say: *Help me.*

At the wedding she turned and looked at their bemused faces. There was no one there but them and Harrow's mother, who was dressed in red and crying. Nora waited for the day to be over and then it was.

She wished someone had told her what living with a man was like. She would not have changed tack but she thought, all the same, a degree of warning would have been good. The musky smell; the stains on the toilet he did not seem to see; the handfuls of tissue she pulled out from down the side of the bed. There were days she thought on what she'd given away. Days she tried to read two books at a time to catch up. Days she went into the city and handed out CVs and saw what little she could get with good marks at school and an attractive husband.

Even then there was never a consideration of going. The shape of him beneath her hands in the morning, the words he said when he was sleepy enough not to think about them, the way he remembered things she told him.

Well, except Harrow had died. Barely a year and she only nineteen, but there it was. She stood next to his mother at the hospital and thought she understood what they were saying except she was certain they were wrong. There wasn't a blood clot in his lung that had, probably, been there since he was born and only now exploded. That was not what had happened. Harrow, she was certain, had died because he decided he loved her after all. He was an eight or a nine and she was a three or a four and the maths of that all added up to Harrow never having been hers to begin with.

At the funeral her parents told her she had to come home, had to grow a life out of whatever she had. They talked about universities and scholarships and jobs in the city and fish in the sea. They were the way she used to be, she saw that now: they were doers. She told them she would get around to it but right now she had to look after Harrow's mother and she hoped they understood.

She was called Sarah and was older than most of the other parents. Nora thought her sort of beautiful; she looked, anyway, a bit like Harrow and held herself in the same unselfconscious way. She'd not seemed to have much comment to make on them marrying but she had, Nora thought, liked her.

Those days Sarah didn't always seem to know where she

was and sometimes she talked about Harrow as if he'd just gone out for a stroll or was running errands. Though these were not things Harrow would ever have done.

Nora did the cooking and cleaned and the rest of the time she read or sat in the sort of stupor that comes from losing the trick of sleeping. She didn't try any more. There wasn't any use trying once it had gone that way.

Nora knew what people said about her. She was up-and-down odd and now Harrow was gone she should move on into a life that more befitted a broad-hipped, glasses-wearing girl who looked – well, it was fine – old before her time.

Part of her always thought Harrow would come back. Maybe she thought it because they were particles entangled. Or because her want was surely strong enough to curse him awake. Or because she'd given up things and – a balancing – needed something in return.

In the end it was none of these things. It was only Sarah.

What are you doing? Nora asked when she found the fragments of tiny animal bones in the bin, tripped over piles of smooth stones in the front garden, tried to make sense of the small dirt offerings: in a cup in the airing cupboard, under her bed, in the bath.

Sarah would not answer her, went out into the garden with her mixing bowl.

When Harrow came back Nora decided she wasn't going to overthink it. Only be a little grateful she hadn't argued harder for a cremation the way she'd wanted to.

There was dirt all over him and he must have – the way they did in the films – dug himself out because there was blood on his hands and most of his nails were cut badly.

Sarah had brought him back, wished him out. Still – she

put the kitchen table between her and him and, scouting around for something to wield, picked up the rolling pin and held it at chest height.

It's all right, Nora said. She held her hand up to Harrow's mouth. He pressed his lips to it hard, leaving a dirt-shaped kiss, and she saw that he was just as relieved as she was.

Let's run a bath, she said. He'll be fine when he's clean.

She took off his suit in the bathroom and then poked and prodded till he climbed into the hot water and stood, arms swinging a little. He wouldn't sit down so she got the sponge and scrubbed until he looked as clean as she could manage, then she towelled him down. He didn't say anything, though he followed her motions with his eyes, touched her hands. She didn't say anything either, only waited. Outside the bathroom she could hear Sarah waiting too.

There were signs she could have read off him that she did not see or chose to ignore: his breathing high and a little laboured, as if air didn't work well in him any more; the odd smell of him: like concrete setting or the cold dredged up on riverbanks.

In the morning she turned in the bed and he was looking at her the way he used to across the classroom or as they passed in the hall when everything they were doing was a secret so he could save face. She felt the rise of him against her leg, held him in her fist and moved her hand. A little later, feeling the comfortable known of his hips against hers, she thought that his time away had lost them nothing, had given them only a perspective of loss. A knowledge of absence. Except, when he arched back his head, mouth open, and let out a one-syllabled word, there was a sharp pain in the roof of her mouth. She rolled out from under him. He lay back, one hand under his head, sweat on his forehead and neck.

Are you all right?

She put a hand over her lips, eyes watering, probed the roof of her mouth with her tongue, felt the pulse of ulcers gathering in rings.

What is it?

It was clear now: again the skid of hurt against her teeth at his words. She rocked back off the bed, one hand warding him away, though he followed, dog-like, reaching out. She caught the door in her fist, shut it between them. His voice, coming muffled through the wood, burnt her mouth and eyes.

What is it? Sarah said, coming down the hallway.

Nora watched, clenching her teeth, as the force of Harrow's muffled words started to hit Sarah's face.

The impact of Harrow's language on Sarah seemed much worse than it was on her – a single syllable eliciting vomiting, sentences starting nosebleeds – so Nora took Harrow to the garage and sat with the door pulled closed.

He wrote: *I don't want to.*

She told him she didn't care. Turned the light out so he couldn't see what was happening to her. Gripped him by the wrist and told him what to do.

They tried out all the letters one by one, cycling through the alphabet twice until she dug her nails hard into his palms and then he was quiet. They worked through nouns, verbs, adjectives. She made him try out adverbs, pronouns and prepositions. She tested herself by waiting for pain, noting down the area and velocity at which it came. When a word seemed to elicit less pain or appear in an area which seemed less extreme (for example her arms or legs as opposed to her face or torso) she squeezed his hand twice to make him repeat it. Mostly the word repeated would bring on pain in a different area or of a different type and then they would carry on. If the word caused in any way a similar reaction she noted it down.

At first the word 'partial' seemed to have a reaction less extreme than others. This was later proved to be otherwise. At first the phrase 'wanted scrabble she' appeared to elicit pain after a longer than normal waiting period. This too turned out to be incorrect.

But if anyone could fix him it was her.

She caught the neighbour's rabbit on one of its escape trips and brought it down in her arms into the garage.

He wrote: *That's enough. I don't need to speak.*

She held the rabbit, not wriggling, only sniffing a little, in her arms. Come on, she said.

He wrote: *Fuck you backwards with a broomstick.*

She told him to go through his consonants the way they'd done before and she would tell him when to stop. She sat numbly as he did it, holding the rabbit. It fought her. She could feel his words on its body.

Later she went round with the rabbit in a plastic bag, told them she'd found it in the garden.

At the end of the week they caught him trying to jemmy the window with a slat broken off his bed. Sarah went down quickly under the onslaught he unleashed against them – unconnected words, curses, quotes Nora recognised from films, the names of people they'd gone to school with. He only stopped when Nora caught, with her finger, the quick trickle of blood from her own nostril, raised her hand to show him.

Most days, when she woke, she could feel it was too late anyway; his words were in her system like a sickness. She could feel the spiky pressure of letters against her gut, the sticks of Ks and Ts and Ls on her insides. She could hear Sarah coughing as if something, a spark plug or wire, had come loose in her. They were not sleeping in the same bed because – though he never had before – he'd started talking in his sleep.

One morning she made a cup of tea, went and opened the door to the sitting room. He was asleep on the sofa. She tightened her stomach in case of an involuntary syllable, a slipped-out sentence. Asleep he looked as if he were an animal, something quiet and wondering, something beautifully thoughtless. She bent to wake him the way she always used to, a slipped tongue in his ear, but, at his eyes flickering, she panicked, dropped the cup of tea, clapped a hand across his mouth to silence whatever might be coming.

She saw the look in his eyes: reproachful, angry. Tried to kiss it away, wiping the hot tea off him with her hands and mouth, felt only that look trained on her while she did.

The house was now perpetually twilight; all the curtains drawn so nobody would see what had come back to them. She and Harrow spent days on the sofa, pen and paper between them, writing long notes to one another, legs tangled beneath the blanket. Once he wrote: *Tell me about the particles.* Slipped a hand beneath the edge of her dressing gown. Wrote: *How does this feel? What does this feel like?*

She could hear – pretended not to and watched him doing the same – Sarah hacking something up in the bathroom.

Most days were not like that. *I'm trapped.* He wrote:

I'm going fucking mad. She ordered him television box sets; ordered him a running machine which he stood and watched her putting together and then refused to use; ordered him books and exotic food and audio tapes.

Let me go out, he wrote, sat across the kitchen table from her. *I'll wear a hood. Just for an hour. Just for a moment. Nobody will notice.* She shook her head.

She sat and watched him wolfing, restless, about the sitting room. The floor was covered in the spread of half-finished jigsaws, half-played games of Monopoly and Cluedo. Now and then a television programme would be turned on but it only ever lasted a moment before the channel was changed. She watched him doing press-ups on the sitting-room floor or pulling himself up by the lintel of a door and, though she had seen this before, he seemed to do it with a new ease, barely breaking a sweat.

It took another month for the words he wrote to become infected too. Sarah was making a concerted effort to spend time with him, though more and more she looked as if she were emptying out of her body, thinning away to nothing. Nora would leave them alone in the kitchen, listen to the strange tick-over of their conversation: the scratch of Harrow's pen on the paper, the slow answers Sarah gave. (Harrow asked things on the page he would never have asked, or thought to ask, when he was verbal.) She listened to the pauses between his questions and Sarah's answers. At one point she could hear him writing for a long time, the fast sound of the words. She could hear it still as she made three cups of tea, carried them in on a tray. There were red blisters coming up on Sarah's arms, on her chest and face. Harrow had not noticed, was writing and writing with a sort of furious intent, nose almost touching the page. Nora tore it away from him and, for a second, he wrote on the table, the letters etched in.

She put Sarah to bed and then went round the house finding all the scattered pages of his words and pushed them into the bin bag. She tried not to see them, those dense, tight little letters against the sick white of the paper; but by the time she was done, she'd caught sight of enough half-words that she had to rest against the corridor wall, breathing hard.

She took the pages out into the garden. Crossed the back field and balled them up and set fire to them. She stood there till it was done. Stood and wondered if the ash would destroy the crop when it grew. The cold air burnt the rash the pages had raised on her arms and chest.

It doesn't matter, she told him when she went back in. He was still sat at the kitchen table. She picked up the pen and put it in the bin, watched his eyes following her. It doesn't matter. She pressed her nose against the solid bone of his face.

Doesn't it?

She bent double. Straightened with difficulty to look at him. He looked back as if she were a creature he'd never seen before.

They spent the rest of the day at the table devising a system of signs. They came up with hand motions for all the words he cared most about. When they were done he seemed changed, smiling at her. He pointed at himself with one finger, jabbed the finger into the O of his other fist, then pointed at her.

She took off her clothes, laughed as he jerked his hands around, forming signs they hadn't discovered yet, commenting. The impact of his language on her over the weeks was clear. She'd never been bony before but she almost was now, the press of ribs more bruise than anything else, the stretch of cheekbone. She took his clothes off, looked for a change on him. He was not loosening the way she'd thought he might. Instead he seemed bigger, stronger; the muscles defined on his chest. She was – no time to stop the feeling – afraid of him. The mass of him: his hands were the size of books flattened open.

He could have stopped her; he could have done anything he wanted. He only watched with wide, brown eyes; let her ball a sock into his mouth, fasten his wrists to the chair with the handcuffs he'd bought her. She pressed her knees into either side of his body as if she could burrow on in if she tried hard enough. She wanted this to mean: nothing has changed. She wanted this to mean: there are signs for everything we can think of and it's not a language anyone else needs to know.

When she was done she pulled the sock out so she could press her mouth to his. Sat straight to look down at him and, when he smiled, felt the wordless expression rot into her insides, sharp explosions of pain in her mouth and on her hands and face and chest.

She kicked backwards, pressed her knuckles eye-ways so she could not see him. On the floor she fell over the scattered remains of his livings: half-full teacups, board games he'd been playing against himself.

I don't want, he said –

Beneath her foot a plate was broken.

– to hurt you. Each word was an attack and before each word she could feel the thought of it – like an echo preceding its sound.

In the corridor on the way to their room his words brought her down and she went on hands and knees. At the bedroom she pushed the door closed, put her weight against it and put her hands over her ears. She could hear the churn of his brain, the guttering end of half-formed thoughts. Most of them were roars that deafened everything else out of her.

She stuffed the gap at the bottom of the door with T-shirts, played music loud. It did not matter. It did not matter that she could not hear if he spoke, that she'd burnt every fragment of his writing: his thoughts were loud enough to blister, to inch belly-ways and shard outwards.

She'd explained to herself before and – though the words didn't taste as good and fresh as they had that first time – did it again now: you could do anything. There was a coil of rope in the wardrobe. The handcuffs were still in the sitting room; she would have to do without. At the last moment, the click of his thoughts turning in her, she snapped two rungs off a chair, held them together: a wobbly cross. She would cover her bases. There were lines from the Qur'an she'd learnt once; stray phrases from the Torah and the Old Testament that she mouthed over, tried to hold onto.

She closed her eyes and took the hallway blind, not touching the walls. There was the smell – though she had not noticed it before – of something turning bad. She could feel the dull pulse of his living, a sucking heat. Expected, every moment, to come upon a mass of muscle, a mouth poised open. In the bathroom she emptied the cabinet of sleeping pills.

She could hear words from somewhere in the house, loud enough to be spoken though she knew they were not: a jumbled flow of thought syllables. There was blood in the sink when she coughed and a wrench in her arms when she moved.

She knew the plan well. And though there were someone else's thoughts hooked and barbed inside her, she saw the dark passage of where she was going: not a rescue at all, only a stripping away, a cursing back into nothing.

CONTRIBUTORS' BIOGRAPHIES

JAY BARNETT grew up in Macclesfield, Cheshire. He is now based in London, where he completed his Creative Writing MA at Birkbeck. For a decade he has worked in the post room of an investment bank. His work has been broadcast on BBC Radio 4 and has appeared in Hamish Hamilton's *Five Dials* magazine, in Birkbeck's *Mechanics Institute Review* and in *Jawbreakers*, the first National Flash-Fiction Day anthology.

PETER BRADSHAW is an author and journalist and has been chief film critic for the *Guardian* since 1999. He has published three novels, *Lucky Baby Jesus* (1999), *Dr Sweet and His Daughter* (2003) and *Night of Triumph* (2013). He has also written and performed the Radio 4 serial *For One Horrible Moment* and the Sky TV situation comedy *Baddiel's Syndrome*. He is married with a son and lives in London.

ROSALIND BROWN was born in 1987 and grew up in Cambridge. She is a graduate of the University of East Anglia's Creative Writing MA, and now lives and works in Norwich.

KRISHAN COUPLAND's stories and poems have been published in *Ambit*, *Aesthetica*, *Brittle Star*, *Fractured West* and *Litro*. His story 'Days Necrotic' was joint winner of the Manchester Fiction Prize 2011; he has also won the *Bare Fiction* Prize and been shortlisted for the Bristol Short Story Prize, *Wasafiri* New Writing Prize, and *Storgy* short story competition. His work has also been highly commended in the *Harper's Bazaar* short story competition, selected for the Best of the Net Anthology, and nominated for a Pushcart Prize.

CLAIRE DEAN's short stories have been published in *The Best British Short Stories 2011* and 2014, as well as in *Still, Shadows & Tall Trees, Patricide, A cappella Zoo* and as chapbooks by Nightjar Press. Her first collection, *The Museum of Shadows and Reflections* (Unsettling Wonder), with illustrations by Laura Rae, was published in 2016. She lives in Lancashire with her two young sons. Two new stories are forthcoming from Nightjar Press in 2017.

NIVEN GOVINDEN is the author of four novels, most recently *All the Days and Nights*, longlisted for the Folio Prize and shortlisted for the Green Carnation Prize. *Black Bread, White Beer* was selected as one of the Fiction Uncovered titles in 2013. His second novel, *Graffiti My Soul*, is to be filmed. His short stories have been published internationally and his novels have been translated into numerous languages.

FRANÇOISE HARVEY has had work published in *Loss Lit, Bare Fiction, Synaesthesia Magazine* and *Litro*, as well as in the anthologies *The Best New British and Irish Poets 2016* and the *Bristol Short Story Prize Anthology Volume 9*. She has been shortlisted for the Bridport Prize and is one of the founders of short-story collective Literary Salmon.

ANDREW MICHAEL HURLEY is the author of two short story collections, *Cages* and *The Unusual Death of Julie Christie*. His first novel, *The Loney*, was originally published in 2014 by Tartarus Press and then by John Murray a year later, after which it won the 2015 Costa First Novel award and the 2016 British Book Industry award for Debut Novel and Book of the Year. He lives in Lancashire with his family and teaches creative writing at Manchester Metropolitan University's Manchester Writing School. His second novel, *Devil's Day*, will be published by John Murray in autumn 2017.

DAISY JOHNSON was born in 1990 and currently lives in Oxford. Her short fiction has appeared in the *Boston Review* and the *Warwick Review*, among others. In 2014, she was the recipient of the AM Heath prize. *Fen* is her first collection of stories. Her debut novel will be published by Jonathan Cape in 2018.

JAMES KELMAN was shortlisted for the Booker Prize in 1989 with *A Disaffection*, which also won the James Tait Black Memorial Prize for Fiction. He went on to win the Booker Prize five years later with *How Late it Was, How Late*, before being shortlisted for the Man Booker International Prize in 2009 and 2011. His latest book is *Dirt Road* (Canongate). A new collection of short stories is forthcoming.

GISELLE LEEB grew up in South Africa and lives in Nottingham, where she works as a web developer when she is not writing. Her short stories have appeared in *Ambit*, *Mslexia*, *Lady Churchill's Rosebud Wristlet*, *Litro*, *Bare Fiction* and elsewhere. In 2016, she won third prize for short fiction in both the Elbow Room and Aurora competitions and was shortlisted for the Bridport Prize. She has recently become an assistant editor at *Reckoning*. She tweets as @gisellekleeb and maintains a website at http://giselleleeb.com.

VESNA MAIN was born in Zagreb, Croatia. She studied comparative literature before obtaining a doctorate from the Shakespeare Institute in Birmingham. She has worked as a journalist, lecturer and teacher. Her two novels are *A Woman With No Clothes On* (Delancey Press, 2008) and *The Reader the Writer* (*Mirador*, 2015). The latter is written entirely in dialogue and one of the characters is a young prostitute who is also the protagonist of 'Safe'. Recent short stories have appeared in *Persimmon Tree* and *Winamop*.

COURTTIA NEWLAND is the author of seven works of fiction. His debut was *The Scholar* and his latest novel, *The Gospel According to Cane*, has been optioned by Cowboy Films. He was nominated for the Impac Dublin Literary Award, the Frank O'Connor Award, the CWA Dagger in the Library Award, the Hurston/Wright Legacy Award and the Theatre 503 Award for playwriting. His short stories have appeared in many anthologies and been broadcast on BBC Radio 4. In 2016 he was awarded the Tayner Barbers Award for science fiction writing and the Roland Rees Busary for playwriting. He is associate lecturer in creative writing at the University of Westminster.

ELIOT NORTH is a doctor and medical educator who lives and works in the north-east of England. She won the EuroStemCell Poetry Competition 2013 and was commended for the Hippocrates Poetry Prize 2014. In 2015 she was commended in the National Poetry Competition. She tweets as @eliot_north and blogs at chekhovwasadoctor.wordpress.com.

IRENOSEN OKOJIE is a writer and arts project manager. Her debut novel, *Butterfly Fish*, won a Betty Trask award and was shortlisted for an Edinburgh International Book Festival First Book Award. Her work has been featured in the *Observer*, *Guardian* and *Huffington Post*, among other publications. Her short stories have been published internationally. She was presented at the London Short Story Festival by Ben Okri as a dynamic writing talent to watch and was featured in the *Evening Standard* magazine as one of London's most exciting new authors. Her short story collection, *Speak Gigantular* (Jacaranda Books), was shortlisted for the Jhalak Prize and in the Saboteur Awards, and longlisted for the Edge Hill Short Story Prize. wwwirenosenokojie.com @IrenosenOkojie

LAURA POCOCK was born in South Wales and is an English teacher living in Leicester. She holds a BA in English from the University of Leicester, and will soon graduate with an MA in Creative Writing from Nottingham Trent University. Laura has written a body of Eco-poetry and enjoys experimenting with the sonnet form. Her short story, 'Recruitment', has recently been published in *Monster*, an anthology of literature by Nottingham writers. She is currently writing a futuristic young adult novel. @_laura_pocock

DAVID ROSE was born in 1949 and spent his working life in the Post Office. His debut story was published in the *Literary Review* (1989), since when he has been widely published in magazines in the UK and Canada. He was joint owner and fiction editor of *Main Street Journal*. He is the author of two novels, *Vault* (2011) and *Meridian* (2015) and one collection, *Posthumous Stories* (2013). Recent stories have appeared in *Gorse*.

DEIRDRE SHANAHAN has had short stories published in *New Writing 5* (Vintage) and *Edgeways* (Flight Press/Spread the Word) as well as journals in Ireland and the US including the *Massachusetts Review* and the *Southern Review*. She has read at Liars League and Word Factory. Her longer fiction has won the Lightship Novel Prize and a bursary from Arts Council England.

SOPHIE WELLSTOOD grew up in rural Warwickshire. Her fiction was first published in 2013, in *Stories for Homes*, an anthology for Shelter. She was longlisted for the Bath Award in 2016 and shortlisted for the Manchester Fiction Prize 2016. Her debut novel won Triskele Books' Big 5 competition and was shortlisted for the 2017 Caledonian Novel Award. She has another story forthcoming in *Stories for Homes Vol 2*, due November 2017. She lives in west London and is working on her second novel and a short story collection.

LARA WILLIAMS is a writer based in Manchester. Her debut collection, *Treats*, was published by Freight Books in 2016; it has been shortlisted for the Republic of Consciousness Prize and longlisted for the Edge Hill Short Story Prize. She writes for the *Guardian*, *Independent*, *TLS* and *Vice* among other publications. She is currently working on a novel and a full-length piece of creative non-fiction.

ACKNOWLEDGEMENTS

'Area of Outstanding Natural Beauty', copyright © Jay Barnett 2016, was first published in *The Mechanics' Institute Review* issue 13 and is reprinted by permission of the author.

'Reunion', copyright © Peter Bradshaw 2016, was first broadcast on BBC Radio 4 and is printed here by permission of the author.

'General Impression of Size and Shape', copyright © Rosalind Brown 2016, was first published in *Lighthouse* issue 11 and is reprinted by permission of the author.

'The Sea in Me', copyright © Krishan Coupland 2016, was first published in *Bare Fiction Magazine* Number 7 and is reprinted by permission of the author.

'Is-and', copyright © Claire Dean 2016, was first published in *Dead Letters* (Titan Books) edited by Conrad Williams, and is reprinted by permission of the author.

'Waves', copyright © Niven Govinden 2016, was first broadcast on BBC Radio 4 and is printed here by permission of the author.

'Never Thought He'd Go', copyright © Françoise Harvey 2016, was first published in *Bristol Short Story Prize Anthology*

Volume 9 (Tangent Books) and is reprinted by permission of the author.

'While the Nightjar Sleeps', copyright © Andrew Michael Hurley 2016, was first published online in *Granta* and is reprinted by permission of the author.

'Language', copyright © Daisy Johnson 2016, was first published in *Fen* (Jonathan Cape) and is reprinted by permission of the author.

'Words and Things to Sip', copyright © James Kelman 2016, was first published in *Gutter* No.15 and is reprinted by permission of the author.

'As You Follow', copyright © Giselle Leeb 2016, was first published online in *Flakes of a Fire* (Aurora Poetry & Short Fiction Award, Writing East Midlands) and is reprinted by permission of the author.

'Safe', copyright © Vesna Main 2016, was first published online in *The Literateur* and is reprinted by permission of the author.

'Reversible', copyright © Courttia Newland 2016, was first published in *Sex & Death* (Faber & Faber) edited by Sarah Hall and Peter Hobbs, and is reprinted by permission of the author.

'This Skin Doesn't Fit Me Any More', copyright © Eliot North 2016, was first published in *Structo 16* and is reprinted by permission of the author.

'Filamo', copyright © Irenosen Okojie 2016, was first published in *An Unreliable Guide to London* (Influx Press) edited by Gary Budden and Kit Caless and is reprinted by permission of the author.

'The Dark Instruments', copyright © Laura Pocock 2016, was first published online at *Manchester Writing Competition* and is reprinted by permission of the author.

'Ariel', copyright © David Rose 2016, was first published in *The End* (Unthank Books) edited by Ashley Stokes, and is reprinted by permission of the author.

'The Wind Calling', copyright © Deirdre Shanahan 2016, was first published in *Prole* issue 21 and is reprinted by permission of the author.

'The First Hard Rain', copyright © Sophie Wellstood 2016, was first published online at *Manchester Writing Competition* and is reprinted by permission of the author.

'Treats', copyright © Lara Williams 2016, was first published in *Treats* (Freight Books) and is reprinted by permission of the author.

RECENT FICTION FROM SALT

RON BUTLIN
Billionaires' Banquet (978-1-78463-100-0)

NEIL CAMPBELL
Sky Hooks (978-1-78463-037-9)

SUE GEE
Trio (978-1-78463-061-4)

CHRISTINA JAMES
Rooted in Dishonour (978-1-78463-089-8)

V.H. LESLIE
Bodies of Water (978-1-78463-071-3)

WYL MENMUIR
The Many (978-1-78463-048-5)

ALISON MOORE
Death and the Seaside (978-1-78463-069-0)

ANNA STOTHARD
The Museum of Cathy (978-1-78463-082-9)

STEPHANIE VICTOIRE
The Other World, It Whispers (978-1-78463-085-0)

This book has been typeset by
SALT PUBLISHING LIMITED
using Neacademia, a font designed by Sergei Egorov
for the Rosetta Type Foundry in the Czech Republic.
It is manufactured using Creamy 70gsm, a Forest
Stewardship Council™ certified paper from Stora Enso's
Anjala Mill in Finland. It was printed and bound by
Clays Limited in Bungay, Suffolk, Great Britain.

LONDON
GREAT BRITAIN
MMXVII